Feng and Russell have made a life together in LA's China-town, except that Feng has no memory of the centuries-old vampire, the imperious, mysterious Banpaia, who abducted then returned them and dozens of other men to their every-day lives.

Feng had fallen in love with Banpaia, who also fell in love with Feng, only to allow the man he'd chosen to be his life mate to return to Earth and try to live a human existence. As Feng's happiness and very life force ebbs away each day, Russell is growing stronger. He remembers the great vampire and uses his memories to great manga. Time may be growing short for an increasingly despondent Feng unless he can re-member his one true love and go to him willingly, before the next Halloween . . .

This book has been previously published.

Ghost Flower
Copyright © 2020 A.J. Llewellyn and D.J. Manly
ISBN: 978-1-4874-3117-4
Cover art by Martine Jardin

Published by eXtasy Books Inc or
Devine Destinies, an imprint of eXtasy Books Inc

Look for us online at:
www.eXtasybooks.com or www.devinedestinies.com

GHOST FLOWER
BANPAIA 2

BY

A.J. LLEWELLYN AND D.J. MANLY

DEDICATION

To the angel and the devil in all of us.

CHAPTER ONE

The dream always started the same way. He saw himself as a little boy, standing on the lapping shorefront of a beach as waves crashed around his ankles. Even in dream, he could feel the deep chill of the foamy water as a little girl beside him blew bubbles into the air. Holding his toy sword aloft, Feng Li ran through the water, chasing the bubbles and hacking them in two, breaking the shimmering shells of rainbows the perfect spheres had formed. The first night he'd dreamed it, he awoke in tears, wondering who the little girl was. His feelings for her, his desire to connect had been the closest he'd come to feeling anything in months.

Now he knew she was his cousin. He longed to touch and talk to her. He needed to know why they had been separated . . . only now the dream kept going. The bubbles he burst left tears. Tears of blood. They fell on his cheeks. He heard voices whispering.

Remember.

He waits for you.

Who waited for him? He loved Russell, his best friend turned lover, but since the strange incident of Halloween almost a year ago, he'd felt so disconnected and isolated from everyone else. He, Russell, and several friends of theirs had all vanished into another realm. When he returned, he could see and taste, think and feel, but he was invisible to others. Especially, his abusive parents. It had scared him at first and even now he didn't fully understand because he'd slowly regained his ability to communicate, to be seen and heard. It didn't feel so good, though.

It didn't feel right.

"Aren't you happy? Russell always asked him. "Isn't it just great to be alive?"

Not really. At the age of twenty-three, Feng hovered between misery and apathy, but never let it show. He caught glimpses of another time and place. *A man . . .*

When Feng thought of him, his heart filled with joy, inexplicable wholeness that kept him buoyant for days. He turned in his sleep, aware of Russell's even breathing beside him. Good. He was asleep.

Feng returned to the dream, seeing drops of blood falling from the bubbles his cousin had blown and he had destroyed. The blood fell on his cheeks and down to his feet.

Feet. He suddenly became aware of dancing feet. A row of women in beautiful, long, pale green dresses with over-sized sleeves began dancing and singing in front of him. Their moves were so graceful but so often extended it looked as if they might be marionettes on the verge of falling. The music was whimsical, their steps entrancing when he caught glimpses of them under the sweep of their gowns.

His gaze flew up into the face of a beautiful young woman. He knew her. And she knew him. With each swirl of her long sleeves, she aged before his eyes.

Mrs. Wei!

Who was Mrs. Wei? He searched his memory. It was just there. Just out of reach. He knew she was dead. He knew he missed her. He begged her not to leave him. For the second time in three nights, his heart, his feelings of love, were coming back to him. He knew he missed Mrs. Wei dreadfully.

And then he remembered—he'd found her dead body. In life, she'd been a famous *ta ge* dancer as a young woman. Then she'd aged. Her movements as he watched were graceful and gorgeous. She was no longer in pain. She charmed and touched him. But how did he know her?

The woman and all those around her formed a pattern like petals, their skirts billowing with slashes of crimson as they danced in small, tight circles. They sang like angels.

Angels!

Remember!

Mrs. Wei stepped forward. "You must return to him. You must remember. You must go back. His sacrifice is too great. You must return when the ghost flower blossoms."

"No!" he yelled as one by one the women popped and disappeared, small rainbows on his soul. He heard their voices still singing in perfect harmony. Tears ran down his cheeks. *Don't leave me. Tell me what to remember!* He longed to shout this out, but the words stuck like dry rice in his throat.

He awoke suddenly, realizing this song was on the radio. Disappointment shook his bones. She had been real. She had loved him. He was certain of that. And what the heck was a ghost flower?

Warm hands moved over his belly and chest. Russell. He'd been so closed to the man for weeks now. He tried not to stiffen as Russell kissed the back of Feng's neck, nuzzling him. He tried to relax. He loved Russell, really he did, but it had morphed into a different kind of love.

Halloween was only days away. He wondered what had happened to Ki, the man he'd had a crush on until he met . . . met . . . whom had he met? He drew a blank.

Russell was hard and obviously excited because he was humping Feng's ass cheeks now, his glistening cockhead beating an insistent tattoo against Feng's crack. Feng didn't want to sigh and bit down on the urge, in spite of his feelings of restlessness. He was surprised how wet Russell was, his cock leaking before they'd even started.

Giving the guy head was less intrusive than taking him up the ass. In the past, Feng had loved getting fucked. The sounds and smells of early morning sex inflamed his soul, giving heat to his dormant fantasies.

That's what it was! How could he have forgotten? His mind had dried up since his return. It was a desert of the soul. No dreams, no idyll. He could give Russell what he wanted in exchange for information. Feng turned around swiftly, one eye on the time. Six-forty in the morning. The red lanterns of LA's Chinatown which swung high outside their windows were still alight, giving Feng a sense of comfort. There was something about them he knew he should remember.

He just didn't know what.

Sex would be over in fifteen minutes. Russell always took very cold showers with salt-soap and birch branches for exactly three minutes each morning. Then he walked over the cobblestone path to the old Chinatown Square to the comic bookstore he'd taken over almost as soon as they'd returned from their strange sojourn a year ago.

In decades past, it had been a ginseng store and the smell still permeated the old quarter. Sometimes, Russell pretended their journey to the other side never happened. Sometimes, he remembered a lot more than he cared to admit. Feng knew this because Russell, who'd longed to be a manga artist, had caved in to the god of money and worked a 'necessary' job instead of following his passion.

Once he came back, he pursued his art, literally. He'd started producing graphic novels that were, frankly, very weird. In them, Russell seemed to pine for a place, some . . . sanctuary. Hey, maybe they weren't so different after all. Russell's comics were about Russell, a boy, who lived in a fantasy world.

He once told Feng that his inspiration had been Feng himself. But Feng couldn't remember being in a fantasy world. Ever. And he remembered nothing of his life before he died.

Died? What made him think that? The idea didn't panic him . . . it just seemed . . . unreal. And of course, it was. Except that lately Russel's comic books reflected more and more glimmers of what had happened to them in their adventures on what Feng had begun to think of as *the other side.*

He moved around so his mouth captured Russell's cock in one, long, fluid motion. Gazing up to watch his lover through his half-closed eyes, Feng saw the look of surprise on Russell's face. Feng had been so disinterested for weeks and now, he knew, Russell was ecstatic.

"Oh, baby," he said, threading his hands through Feng's hair. Feng sucked Russell, giving it all he had. He had questions to ask and he was convinced Russell had the answers. A little sugar from Feng and it felt certain Russell would give him the answers he needed.

He ticked them off in his mind. Who is the man who haunts my dreams? Why can't I see his face but why do I feel . . . no, I know he loves me? What is a ghost flower? Who is Mrs. Wei? Why am I excited that Halloween is coming? Does it have something to do with . . . him?

Feng felt Russell's excitement and kept his throat open, his lips tight, giving the man a mind-blowing thrill. Russell always tasted good. His lover fell back against the bed, his mouth softer in repose. He'd been so tense with Feng lately. Amazing what a bit of sex could do to a man.

"Shower with me," Russell said, but Feng balked. He saw no pleasure or real medicinal value in using the salt-soap and flogging himself with tree branches, but Russell swore by these things. Feng lingered in bed, wanting to clean his teeth and rinse his mouth as soon as Russell walked out the door. Russell came back, naked, and wet, looking cheerful, his skin blush-pink from the workout he'd given it with the birch branches. He looked healthy and glowing, his smile cheerful. Maybe Feng should consider beating himself up a little. Maybe it would perk him up. Russell was always so damned chipper these days, except for the area of their sex life.

Russell toweled off quickly, dressing in his usual jeans and long-sleeved gray Gap sweater. Russell wore a lot of gray lately. His comic books were gray, too. He did not write the series, called *Shades of Gray* under his own name. He just used initials. R.B. His illustrations were dark, his stories also dark. His character, Russell, was on a metaphysical journey to himself. Most of the young kids who came to the store picked up his books and flicked through them, impressed with his art. They admired his vision and his scope.

Feng did, too. Russell spent hours working on his art. The kids found him an interesting guy and were fascinated by his theory of there being forty-one shades of gray, but lost interest in his storyline. Feng read the comic books as they came out, trying to understand Russell's happiness. Feng wished some of that for himself. As far as he could make out, Russell was happy on the surface, but his sense of isolation was deeply imbedded in the pages of *Shades of Gray*.

"Wait for me, I'm coming with you," Feng said. Russell must have been in a good mood. He nodded and sat on the bed sketching in his leather-bound book of parchment paper as Feng showered and cleaned his teeth. He looked at his face in the mirror. He missed dreaming and longed to return to . . . something feather-light flickered across his skin.

He turned around, his entire body alight.

For him.

Feng missed him so much. Whoever the hell he was . . .

Russell wondered why Feng was being so nice this morning. As they walked over to the store, they sipped takeout cups of coffee. Russell had to keep his emotions in check. He was certain Feng was starting to remember what happened. Russell couldn't afford for that to happen. The guy had been as moody as all hell since they came back from the vampire's lair, but Russell had taken comfort in knowing Feng needed him. Somehow, much of his memory had gone. He seemed happy enough, sometimes, but other times, Russell sensed the sincere despair in his lover. He worried. They said the vampire came once every two hundred years to claim a mate, but Russell had a weird feeling Banpaia had chosen the wrong mate.

He had the strange feeling Feng had wanted to return to be with Russell, to have a chance at life. He often told Feng that *Shades of Gray* was inspired by Feng and it was, except that he pretended that the search for self was his own. But it wasn't. It was Feng's.

All the other men who'd been seduced by Banpaia seemed to have thrived since their return. Russell saw them blossoming, living fulfilling lives for the most part. Feng had always been kind of depressed. Now it was worse because he tried so hard to hide it.

Russell saw improvements in his lover. Feng no longer spoke to his parents and therefore didn't take their abuse anymore. He didn't seem to fantasize about secret worlds and obsess over comic-book stories. He dutifully read *Shades of Gray* and made some incisive comments, but he wasn't really . . . Feng.

As they walked into the store, his lover's shiny head bent over a shipment of new graphic novels. Feng was always great about helping him opening pallets and displaying the latest books for the customers. It surprised Russell that Feng, who'd always been so obsessed with the latest manga, had stopped reading them since their return. He read Russell's books dutifully. But that was it, duty. He noticed Feng opening one packet, taking out the latest *Phoenix Wright: Ace Detective* novels and . . . staring at them. Why was he showing interest in these books?

Feng suddenly glanced up at him. "I dreamed about Mrs.

Wei last night." His gaze fell again, and Feng lapsed into silence. It so often happened with him and Russell wanted to engage him in conversation. Feng never mentioned Mrs. Wei anymore, but then her passing had been traumatic for his lover. She was the closest thing to a mother Feng had ever had.

"Well," Russell said, as he unpacked more books. "It's not surprising really, with her killer being on trial and everything. It's a good thing they haven't called you up to take the stand." He paused, gazing at Feng. "They haven't, have they?"

Feng shook his head, his fingers running along the margins of the illustrations in his hand. His thumb stroked the brilliant blue of Phoenix Wright's blue business suit. The colors in this book were a strong contrast with Russell's bleak canvas. Everything since he'd left Tenshi seemed gray. He had a feeling it did for Feng as well, but Feng needed to snap out of his doldrums. He couldn't wallow in misery forever.

They'd all lost Tenshi. Except for stupid Ki. Russell knew that Tenshi had given up a lot to allow Feng to return to Earth for him. The only problem was that Russell felt as if sometimes Feng regretted his decision. They'd all loved and lost Tenshi. The trick was to be grateful for having been able to touch the sun and carry on with their lives.

Feng stood, without finishing to help unpack the books.

"I gotta go," he said.

"Where to?" Russell asked. He regretted it instantly. He knew that Feng was probably going to return to that dreary hotel and take back his old job. They'd fired him when Mrs. Wei died, not that it was Feng's fault, but the owner of the hotel had no idea how good Feng was at his job. Feng was sweet. He was calm. He was very good with people. The owner of the hotel, a pushy guy who called himself Mr. Huang, had called their landline several times, begging Feng to come back. Russell had deleted all the messages . . . or so he thought.

Russell worried about Feng going back there. When Mrs. Wei had been murdered, the police suspected Feng initially and made no bones about it. This had affected Feng terribly of course, and the owner jumped in saying a large sum money had been stolen, too. Mrs. Wei's daughter had refuted this, and it had since been proven that no money had disappeared and, of course, that Feng had not murdered the elderly woman he cherished. Russell knew Feng had tried to kill himself by throwing himself into the path of a train. He'd been saved by a strange, dark angel they both had come to know as the ancient vampire, or *banpaia* as they said in Japanese. Tenshi had seduced and abducted many men, who had all returned. Just Russell's luck to get the one guy that couldn't get over losing Tenshi.

When Feng said nothing, Russell patted his shoulder. "No worries, have fun."

Feng kissed his cheek and walked out the door. Russell regretted his sarcastic tone. Feng was so easily hurt these days. He felt terrible all of a sudden. How awful for poor Feng that he was dreaming about Mrs. Wei. It must have been a terrible shock to find her covered in blood. The killer's trial had just started on TV a few days ago, but Russell had taken pains to change channels as soon as his face appeared, and he'd done a good job of keeping local papers away from Feng's reach.

Not that Feng noticed. He didn't read much anymore. Russell had no idea what his lover did with his time, but just as he was about to chase after him, an old, old man walked in and Russell had no choice but to attend him.

He stepped back inside, not happy that the old man, Mr. Sun wrestled with the small pieces of information that Russell had given him.

Mrs. Wei had been real. He'd found her body. She'd been murdered and the trial was happening now. Why hadn't he been asked to give testimony? Feng walked away from the comic bookstore, aware of that nasty old goat, Mr. Sun rushing past him to get inside. In Feng's opinion, Russell had made a deal with the devil in taking over the comic bookstore. In exchange for nominal rent, Mr. Sun was allowed full use of the room upstairs, where he ran a bookie joint, and, Russell had confided, booked clients for prostitutes working at two hotel rooms in the Cecil Hotel on Main Street.

He felt relief, however, because Russell had started to follow him, probably to keep asking questions. *Where are you going? What are you doing?*

Feng had taken a job four days a week stacking returned books, DVDs, and books on CD, at the Chinatown library across the road on Hill Street. He hadn't told Russell because Russell would ask too many questions. He would probably also give him a hard time about money, even though Feng paid his share of all the bills.

He was far too early for work now, but when he saw one of the librarians entering the building through the staff door, he hurried across the road.

"Tina!" He waved to her and she smiled back, holding the door for him.

"You're like . . . three hours early," she said.

"I know it." He nodded. "I need to use a computer and to—"

"Hold on," she said. "I have to turn off the alarm." She closed the door on him, and he stood outside, waiting. When she returned, she held it open for him and let him inside.

He repeated his request for the use of a computer.

"I can't turn on the library computers because they're all calibrated to be turned on at ten o'clock, and of course they're booked solid for the whole day. If you're not going to be long, you can use one of the librarian's computers."

"Oh, that would be great, thanks!"

She pointed him to an empty desk, and he fired up the computer as Tina busied herself making coffee and getting her labels and barcodes ready for new books.

He Googled Mrs. Wei and murder trial and up popped a bunch of story threads. He read everything. There was little mention of him, but suddenly he glimpsed a face he remembered. Detective Stevens. Memories flooded back of Stevens grilling him, accusing him. Feng sat back in the chair, the hard movement making his takeout coffee cup topple on the desk beside him. He grabbed it before it could slosh liquid anywhere.

Now it all made sense! Several months ago, Detective Stevens had approached him on the street with another man in a suit. They had insisted on talking to him. The second man had said he was an attorney with the mayor's office. At least, that's what Feng thought the man had said. They had followed him up to the apartment he shared with Russell. Stevens had banged on about mistakes being made and Feng's reputation being so important.

"I never meant for you to be accused in the media. Leaks might have been made," Stevens said. "And then you tried to kill yourself. Mr. Lee, that was never my intention. I just wanted to catch the guy that brutally murdered a nice, old lady."

Stevens had said, "How did you survive jumping in front of the train. Man, it looked like you were a goner! I saw the security tape. The train driver still hasn't been able to go back to work. He thought he'd killed you. What saved you?"

An angel. Feng saw him in shadows now. His name lingered in the back of his throat, rendering him mute. To say or think his name would mean pain. More pain.

Why did I leave him?

Feng hadn't said much to Stevens or the other man. He'd been afraid of looking stupid. How could he say he'd

11

forgotten everything? The attorney man had passed him a certified check for a hundred-thousand dollars. Feng had been stupefied to receive a check for so much money. In his wallet, he'd had a driver's license, college ID and a Bank of America ATM card. He had the strong feeling he'd never seen so much money in his life and immediately signed the gazillion papers the men had made him sign. He'd deposited the check immediately. He'd forgotten his pin number for his account but the people at the bank helped him set up a new one.

At the college he'd been attending, he found he was a good student with two credits to go, then he could apply for Librarianship. Being around books was what he wanted.

He'd started work at the library as a volunteer, but they had insisted he should get paid after a few months. Feng stared at a photo of Xiu Teng, Mrs. Wei's killer. The man's face seemed familiar, but Feng couldn't readily identify him. He read the article. It said that she'd been murdered at the Cedar House hotel. Feng knew that he'd worked there, because Stevens had told him this. He'd seen the hotel before, and he'd go over there now and see what feelings he got. He wished he had a memory of it. He had nothing.

Nothing . . .

That dear old lady had been murdered by a hotel guest. Feng remembered finding her. He remembered how badly he felt. He stared at the image of Xiu Teng. Why didn't he remember him? Thoughts came back. Ugly, slashing memories he wished would remain dormant.

People thought I did it. Even the creep who owned the place. The only one who spoke up for me was a woman . . . who was she? He struggled to remember.

"You almost done?" Tina asked him. Did you find what you wanted?" She looked over his shoulder. "Oh, you poor thing. At least now the killer has pleaded guilty, there won't be a trial and you won't have to give evidence. I know how traumatic it must have been for you. You never speak of her, but I hear she was a wonderful woman."

"Mrs. Wei . . . was . . ." he couldn't speak. Rage swelled within him. He was afraid he'd shout out that he didn't remember . . . couldn't remember . . .

"Of course she was," Tina said, her voice soothing. Sometimes she spoke to Feng as if he were very stupid or hard of hearing. She enunciated her words and sometimes rolled her eyes at him when she thought he wasn't looking.

Something inside him snapped.

"She was kindness personified and the kindest human being I ever met. She could dance. Did you know that?"

Tina blinked. In the eight months they'd worked together, this was perhaps the longest conversation they'd had.

"A dancer? No. How . . . unusual."

"Not unusual. She was a *ta ge* dancer, in her day." He stood, just as Tina said, "Ta ge? What is that? Is that a fancy word for stripping?"

"No," he said. "Chinese folk dancing."

Tina, who was of full Chinese descent, must have been embarrassed because she went on the attack. "I hope you won't make a habit of coming in early to use the computer, Feng."

He shrugged. "Haven't before, probably won't again." He had a feeling he may not come back and work here again. He didn't really like Tina. He had money to buy a computer, but he didn't want Russell asking questions. He didn't want to tell his lover he had money because . . . well, because he was too embarrassed to tell him he didn't exactly know why he had it.

Outside the library, he watched gray clouds skitter across the sky. If Russell were to draw the clouds, he wondered which shade of gray he would use. Feng stared upward. He'd personally choose cadet gray, for its touch of blue. He smiled up at the sky. It was a pretty shade of gray.

Shades of Gray. He understood why Russell called his series by this name. Since their return from what Russell sometimes insisted was a shared dream, nothing was as bright or beautiful anymore. Feng realized now he'd chosen the library in which to hide because it was quiet. It had suited him because he hadn't wanted to talk. Now, he longed to talk, to discuss his ideas. He was afraid to mention them to Russell, who always got upset when Feng even *mentioned* their time on the other side. A lot of time had lapsed since he'd talked to some of the others who'd disappeared. He wondered how they felt.

He thought about walking over to the Cedar House hotel, but instead, he felt like wandering, enjoying his new-found spark. It was as if a different kind of flower had started to bloom within him. Ghost flower. Mrs. Wei had told him he must return when it bloomed. He'd meant to Google ghost flower but had been interrupted by Tina.

Never mind. Some things he had to find out for himself.

He walked down Hill Street, happy to see so many red lanterns coming out for Halloween. Families rushed by with shopping bags and cheap Chinese brooms. A woman brandishing a cinnamon broom brushed past him. He paused to inhale the spicy scent. He stood outside a grocery store with its barbecued Peking ducks hanging from hooks in the window. It always upset him to see the strangled birds, their bent and twisted heads turned at odd angles, their blackened, unseeing eyes shriveled up.

Feng took a sharp breath. Beside him in the window was the reflection of a man.

It was him.

In joy, he turned, but nobody was there. He turned back again. The reflection was gone. He was remembering. He would remember *him*. He would call his name. He would. He had to.

In a sudden wash of despair, Feng dropped his head, and wept.

CHAPTER TWO

Banpaia. Tenshi. Eternal love. Return to me.

Tenshi backed away from the window, surprised when the love of his life noticed his reflection. He'd been following Feng for days, dismayed to see how unhappy the most beautiful man in the world was. He'd shadowed Feng without ever getting too close, but he couldn't help himself. He'd missed Feng so much and had to find a way to reach him, to help him remember.

I should never have let him leave. None of this would have happened. It's all my fault.

Tenshi had uttered these words, *Banpaia. Tenshi. Eternal love. Return to me,* over and over again to Feng. Something had shifted today, and Tenshi felt encouraged. Maybe he could wait a little longer and see if Feng remembered him, remembered their love, and came to him.

He'd stood so close to Feng he could smell his skin. He could have reached his tongue out and licked . . . bitten him, tasted his pure blood. He missed Feng so much. The price Tenshi had paid had been high. He could no longer access some of his higher rooms and tired easily. If Feng were to return to him, he feared he might be disgraced, that he wouldn't be able to impress him with dazzling feats of flight and hours and hours of luxurious sex. It had been so hard to watch Feng pleasure Russell, but it had appeased his angry spirit that Feng had resisted allowing the man to fuck him.

Russell. What the hell would they do with him?

Tenshi followed a distracted Feng from a distance.

Together, neither would feel lonely, or lost. He had known Feng wouldn't cope very well back on the earthly side of the veil, but he'd had no choice. The *Banpaia's* lover had to come to him of his own accord.

Feng turned and stopped, staring straight through him.

Banpaia. Tenshi. Eternal love. Return to me.

This mantra had given Tenshi so much strength since he'd returned to Chinatown in search of what was his. It distressed him that Feng had isolated himself, but for selfish reasons, it seemed best. He loved Feng so much and could give him the happiness he so needed and deserved. Tenshi shuddered when he thought about how close he had come to killing Ki, an odious young man who wasn't a fair trade for the noble Feng.

At least he had given Feng the gift of not needing to enable his abusive parents anymore. He'd followed Feng sporadically upon his return to Earth, making him invisible to those who might hurt him, but now, Feng's fragility threatened to hurt him more.

Russell. Tenshi's thoughts cycled back to him. What could he do with him? Tenshi had to make a move fast because unless Feng returned to him by All Hallows Eve, unholy terror would be unleashed. Tenshi had enough self-control not to start killing off humans to slake his thirst for blood. He knew however, that others in his kingdom, without Tenshi being in full control and in a committed partnership, would be able to override him and descend to Earth and start attacking, claiming victims left and right.

He would give Russell another lover. It came to him in that moment, he would give him Ki.

Russell was fed up. Feng's phone was turned off and he hadn't returned a single call or text. Russell had gone home early when the bookies upstairs had started to bug him with their opium smoking and stupid betting. They could get loud, especially when they were stoned.

Sometimes he thought Feng had the right idea distancing himself from people. Russell had gone through Feng's private papers expecting to find a diary . . . drawings . . . anything.

Something made him go through Feng's papers. He'd been surprised to find there *was* no diary. No drawings. But he was stunned to learn the man had almost a hundred-thousand dollars in his bank account! Where the hell had it come from? Russell began to pace. One part of him tried to reason with himself that it wasn't important. It wasn't *millions*. And it was, after all, Feng's money.

Feng paid his way and even sprang for dinner on the rare occasions he showed interest in food. Feng had become a bore because he wasn't interested in *anything*. The money sure explained why Feng didn't seem anxious about working. He'd mentioned he had a parttime job and maybe he did. How had he gotten so much money? He had found bank statements going back months and realized the payment had come in a single check. For what?

He fired up his laptop and accessed Feng's bank account. He knew his lover's social security number because it was on the statement. He created an online account. It was scary how easy it was to access Feng's financial records. He typed in the transaction date and stared in disbelief. The check had come from the Los Angeles Police Department.

It must be something to do with Mrs. Wei's murder. He let out a breath. For one scary moment, he thought maybe Feng had been the one who'd stolen his stash of *Banpaia* graphic novels and sold them all.

In reality, he'd found out months ago every copy had disappeared. Vanished. All the guys who'd bought them said the same thing. Some people thought it was a stunt and liked it. He sometimes wondered when a new one would come out.

Now it was almost Halloween, maybe they would again.

Russell wondered about the money and what Feng would do if it suddenly disappeared. He felt something cold at the back of his neck and shivered. It was as if an icy finger had reached out and stroked his nape. He hastily packed all of Feng's belongings back into the old red-lacquered cigar box where Feng kept his treasures. Not that there was much. Russell realized Feng appeared to have no inner life anymore. *How . . . weird.*

He became alarmed. Something . . . someone was in the room with him.

"Tenshi?" he asked aloud, then felt stupid. Of course it wasn't Tenshi. He got up from the dining room table and looked outside the window. Dusk. The color of the sky was . . . battleship gray. Somehow that seemed apt. He was going to have a battle royal with Feng before this night was through, but before that, a little karaoke. Yeah, maybe a little action, too. Feng was being so stingy with sex lately. Who could blame Russell for straying? And anyway, sex was just sex. Not love.

Do I even love Feng anymore?

He threw on an A and F sweater and left the apartment. He walked across Hill Street and turned the corner toward Main. A few blocks and he'd be at the hot new karaoke bar. He'd become a really popular performer there lately. He couldn't shake the icy feeling at his neck. He shook himself.

Get a grip on reality, guy.

A few blocks over on First Street, he climbed the stairs to Club Koko and found a cluster of adoring fans waiting for him.

"Mangaka!" they shouted as soon as they saw him. Patrons lining the bar began banging their glasses on the countertop. Everyone wanted to buy him drinks. Being a successful artist had its perks. He kept this part of his life hidden from Feng, partly because he didn't want Feng knowing he had all these fans that paid him big money for private artwork. All his paintings were of the *Banpaia*. The fans loved them, but they secretly bothered Russell because as good as he was, he couldn't capture the great vampire's beauty and magic. The pieces were static and in no way did him justice.

But the fans didn't know. They'd heard about *Banpaia*. They all asked what had happened to the graphic novels. Was it true they all just . . . vanished?

Russell shook hands with a couple of guys who begged him to let them buy him a beer. He agreed to a tall glass of Sapporo because he knew the club catered to a Japanese clientele and their national beer wouldn't be watered down.

A couple of guys sidled over to him. Somebody dropped a kiss on his cheek. Vincent. Russell was pleased to see him. Vincent had been one of the first men taken by the *Banpaia* a year ago and like Russell seemed to thrive from the experience. They rarely talked about it, but Vincent made the most of having vanished and coming home. He was the token Asian actor on a TV crime series and had a huge national ad running for a new line of egg rolls. The money he'd made had afforded him a swanky new apartment in one of the new neomodern loft buildings down on Alameda Street.

Russell felt a pang of envy watching the way Cool Vince splashed his money around. He thought about his own faded apartment in Chinatown. In truth, he loved it and treasured the history of his crumbling piece of genuine architectural history, but Vincent had all the perks and none of the . . . angst of their unusual experience. Russell wondered about that. Though their abduction tied them together, a strong competitive streak ran through both men.

Vincent cupped the back of Russell's head with an insistent hand and kissed him hard. On the lips.

There had been a lull in the music, but a loud disco beat began to thrum through the club, replaced by the morose, opening strains of *MacArthur Park*. What a throwback to the good ol' days of disco! Russell balked when Vincent kissed him, but he was aware that people had stopped watching him and all eyes had turned toward the stage where someone who looked familiar began singing the Donna Summer classic, dressed like the singer, complete with a curly black wig. The crowd went wild.

"Who is that?" Russell asked Vincent.

"You remember Joby, don't you?"

"No. He's sensation. Really beautiful."

As he began to sing and gyrate to the full disco beat, the audience went nuts. Damn. Joby looked good in a red mini dress and high heels.

"He moonlights, some fancy lawyer now I hear."

Russell was grateful to no longer be the center of attention. He really wanted to just linger and watch, but with Vincent trying to paw him, he had to get away. Coming here again had been a mistake. He should *never* have fooled around with Vincent the last time he came here. He'd almost confessed to Feng that he'd cheated but feared losing his lover. And besides, it was just head. Getting and giving head wasn't fucking, right?

He'd wanted to confess, worried that Vincent would blab. Maybe telling Feng himself could dull what would undoubtedly be a savage blow. It didn't need to be the end of their relationship. He realized now, too late, as Vincent pressed up against him at the bar, covering Russell's mouth with his that Vincent wanted everyone to know about them. Vincent had no respect for Russell or his relationship with Feng.

Sweet, sweet, Feng.

Russell pushed Vincent off him and tried to move away. Vincent was more forceful this evening. Russell began to panic, just a little. He realized now he'd been really unfair to Feng who'd been traumatized by their return.

Why did I hold out on him? Why did I make him think I didn't remember what happened? Why didn't I let him speak?

No wonder Feng had been silent. He had nowhere to go . . . nobody to turn to.

Feng!

Russell's guilt ate at him for the first time in months. Maybe Feng never told him about his windfall because he didn't know how Russell would take it. He had to speak to him and talk to him. He had to make Feng understand.

He broke away from Vincent at last, but the other man grabbed him and dragged him to one of the back rooms. Russell's protests died on his lips as Vincent pushed him against a dark corner of a private room, opened Russell's fly, dropped to his knees, and began to suck his cock.

Oh, boy.

Vincent was a consummate cocks-man. He sucked cock like nobody else, except . . . *Banpaia.*

Russell could have pushed him away. He could have walked out of here and gone straight home to Feng. But he didn't. He wanted to get his cock sucked. For some reason, when Russell closed his eyes, he could see *Banpaia's* face. He could see every loving detail as if the man were right here. How come when he was having sex, he saw the great vampire's eyes so clearly?

He longed to draw as Vincent cradled Russell's balls with one hand, stroking his rigid shaft in time with his sucking mouth with the other. Feng gave good head, too, but he was so stingy with his affections these days.

Oh . . . no . . . did Feng suspect? Did he know? These questions flew into Russell's mind and stayed there, a painful splinter on his soul.

He opened his eyes as his cock did things of its own accord, seeking asylum in Vincent's tight mouth.

Russell gasped. Vincent was no longer sucking him. Vincent lay on the floor in a heap. The man on his knees giving him such a great workout was none other than . . . *Banpaia.*

Tenshi came off Russell's cock for a moment. "Miss me?" he asked.

Russell nodded, as if in a trance.

"I want to draw you," Russell whispered. "I've missed your eyes."

Tenshi went back to sucking Russell's cock. Vincent lay beside them, sleeping. He let out a small moan. When Tenshi had overpowered him and knocked him out, he'd given the man dreams. Tenshi rose, releasing Russell's cock.

He stood, face to face with Russell, trying hard to hide his disgust. Feng had trusted Russell and Russell had fallen so short of the mark.

For a moment, he hesitated, fighting the urge to bite the man and drain his lifeforce completely.

He was surprised when Russell turned his head, begging for Tenshi to bite him.

"I miss your teeth!"

Was the man kidding? Vincent moaned in his sleep. Tenshi flicked a gaze toward him, then returned his attention to Russell. He kissed him, his tongue moving against Russell's in long, languid strokes. He'd forgotten how sensual Russell could be, so consumed with Feng had he been. Tenshi gave Russell a slow, erotic kiss, pressed closely to him, his fingers remaining on Russell's burgeoning erection.

The crowd went wild in the main room as Joby began singing another song. He'd blossomed like a crazy, carnival flower since returning to his life.

Tenshi took his mouth away from Russell, turning the man's head, aware of the pulsing beat in Russell's throat. It pleased him that Russell gave himself up so easily . . .willingly. Made the blood taste so much sweeter. He drank deeply, Russell's heartbeats echoing in Tenshi's head. As soon as the pattern faltered, he stopped, gulping down the blood. He swallowed hard, slicking the puncture wounds closed with his tongue.

Russell thrashed against the wall in throes of near orgasm. Tenshi dropped to his knees, capturing the man's leaking cock with his lips. He began to suck in earnest, Russell's hands flying to Tenshi's head holding him exactly where he wanted him. Tenshi slipped one hand between Russell's ass cheeks, stroking coaxing the man's thighs to part. As Russell's ass cheeks relaxed, Tenshi's fingers stroked along Russell's crack. Russell moaned.

Tenshi managed to turn Russell around so that the man was facing the wall, away from him. Tenshi pressed his face between Russell's ass cheeks. Russell's stifled moans of pleasure made Tenshi happy. He licked and fingered Russell's hole, trying to insert a finger. The slight pressure alone seemed to send Russell into overdrive. Tenshi turned him around again and slid a finger inside Russell, taking possession of the man's cock again.

Russell trembled with the impact of his pending release; his hands splayed against the wall. Once again, his hands shot to the vampire's head and he came hard, flooding Tenshi's throat.

"Oh, God," Russell whimpered. When he opened his eyes, he was stunned to find that the man cradling his cock in his warm mouth was not Vincent, who sat up on the floor now rubbing his eyes. It wasn't even Tenshi. No, the man who released Russell's cock was . . . Ki.

"Ki!" Russell couldn't believe his eyes.

"Where am I?" Ki asked, his eyes dark with confusion.

Russell stared down at him. "Don't you know?"

Ki remained kneeling on the floor and gazed up at Russell.

"I just remember following you here. Something told me to come."

"You followed me?" Russell shifted his hips and moved away from Ki's face. He rearranged his cock in his pants. The one thing he always hated was packing his guys away after a hot orgasm like that. It seemed to lessen the impact, but he had to get dressed. Anyone could walk in here.

"Hey," Vincent said, getting to his feet. "Did you punch me, man?"

"No." Ki didn't sound certain. He got to his feet, wiping Russell's juices from his lips. Russell noticed a smear of blood across Ki's jaw. Man, it had been so long since he'd seen him, and he'd forgotten what a hottie Ki was.

He helped Ki to his feet. Ki's eyes went from cloudy to bright in seconds.

"Russell?" he asked.

"Yeah, it's me."

Ki looked at him. "What the fuck? Did I just give you a blowjob?"

"Er . . . yeah."

Ki shook his head. "When did I get back?"

"Don't you remember?"

Ki looked confused. "No."

Russell nodded. It had been strange for him and Feng, too. He wouldn't leave Ki in the wilderness though. He'd help him through his strange return. He knew exactly how it felt. It was as if you'd stepped out from a train station, you'd been to a million times before, but nothing was familiar. A scary, alienating feeling.

"You hungry?" Russell asked.

Ki titled his head to one side. "I don't know."

Oh, boy, the guy had it bad. Russell remembered the feeling. Poor Ki. Poor Feng. Wait until he told him that he'd had sex with Vincent. *And* with Ki.

Arsenic and ash gray. These were the shades of gray that swirled across the late afternoon sky right now. Feng had memorized all the shades of gray from Russell's color box. If Russell were here, he'd tell him his thoughts. Well, Russell was here . . . sort of. Feng stood on the corner of First Avenue on the outskirts of Little Tokyo, or J Town as some locals called it. If he crossed the street, he'd be leaving Chinatown and entering J Town. He'd just seen Russell go up the stairs to a club. Clubbing in the early afternoon! What was going on with Russell these days? It wasn't the first time he'd closed the store early and taken off, but Feng couldn't imagine what Russell would be doing in there.

He paused and listened. Karaoke. In the old days, before they left, before they were taken, they'd both loved karaoke, but this club, Koko, the name rang no bells, but the location was familiar. He thought about going inside but realized the area itself was very soothing to him.

I spent a lot of time here. The cafés. He smiled now, remembering snatches, in color, wow, wait until he told Russell his sense of color was returning! He remembered coming to the Korean cafés and drinking tea and coffee before heading to work.

Work . . . where had he worked? Mrs. Wei had been murdered at the Cedar House Hotel. Maybe it was there. Yes, definitely there. He did not want to go there. He wanted to remember her dancing. Not covered in blood.

His head dropped as the memory leapt into his brain of finding her. His despair. He'd had no idea the killer was a guest. A difficult guest. He remembered now.

"Feng?"

He turned. A pretty, honey-haired woman with a young boy standing beside her, smiled at him. She looked ecstatic to see him.

"Feng! It is you! Oh, I'm so glad to see you!" She rushed toward him, but the little boy, who must have been about eleven or twelve, blew past her and threw himself into Feng's arms.

It was the first time in a whole year that somebody had touched him, and it wasn't for sex. For a moment, Feng hesitated, the woman's look of concern etching her brow. He couldn't remember either of them, but they seemed to know him.

He wrapped his arms around the child and hugged him.

"I've missed you so much!" the boy said, his tears muffled by Feng's sweater.

Feng fought off his own tears. He remembered them now.

"Antonio." Feng remembered the child's name. He and his mom had been part-time residents of the Cedar House hotel. They had been homeless as a result of domestic violence. With the California state law's complicated rules, they had been able to live in a homeless shelter where the mother . . . what was her name . . .had been taking computer classes. Every thirty days, she and Antonio were forced to leave the shelter and seek residence elsewhere.

Angie. Her name was Angie Montoya. Feng almost shouted her name he was so pleased to have remembered it.

Her indulgent smile as she watched Feng's tender stroking of her little boy's head turned to laughter.

"It's been a long time. How are you, Feng? You look so skinny. Don't you eat?"

"When I remember." He smiled down at Antonio who had pulled a comic book out of his backpack.

"I've been reading all the books you gave me. I've kept them all!"

Feng's heart almost broke. He had no real memory of any of them, but it was obvious Antonio had real pride in his treasures. The comic books were at least a year old.

"No new ones?" he asked.

"No," Angie told him. "I can't really afford them. We get some from the library, but these are his favorites."

"Are you still in school?"

"No! I graduated and I work for a chiropractor on Fourth Street." Angie stepped forward and hugged him. "We have semi-permanent family housing with some other families we knew from the shelter. The rent is low and as long as I keep my job, I can live there for the next twelve months. Then they'll review my case and maybe help me with something long-term."

"That's fantastic," Feng said, genuinely happy for them both.

"We were about to grab a snack. Care to join us?" Angie asked.

"Yeah!" Antonio seemed excited now. "Come with us, Feng."

He accompanied them to a Korean café he vaguely remembered from the bamboo-pattern tablecloths. He inhaled the scent of fresh peanut-butter, his mouth watering as Angie ordered *go mo bang* for them all. She and Feng asked for coffee, Antonio for apple juice. He colored a drawing in his exercise book.'

"My son wants to be a mangaka," Angie told him.

"He has real talent." Feng remembered he had a box of colored pencils in his backpack and dug into it for them. He'd never used them. He just liked knowing he had the colors at his fingertips whenever he was feeling . . . gray.

"You introduced us to those buns," she said, grinning.

Feng couldn't remember that. He did remember Mrs. Wei constantly feeding him because he was broke.

Where did my money go? Oh . . . my parents. I gave them every-thing. He had a sudden flash of Mrs. Wei giving him money to buy his comic books. He passed Antonio the box of colors.

"They're expensive," Angie said. "You can't give him these."

"I can and I want to. They're Japanese soft art crayons. Perfect for shading." A copy of *Shades of Gray* fell from his backpack. Antonio paused in opening the pencils, his eyes alight with excitement.

"You have a new comic?" He craned his neck to see the title. "Oh, I heard about this book. Russell writes these, doesn't he?"

Feng couldn't remember introducing Russell to the boy, but since Antonio seemed to know him, he said yes. Russell pretended his books were written anonymously but almost everyone knew Russell wrote them.

"My friend Billy got the first one. "

"Would you like to have this?"

The boy hesitated. "Billy says the new books are strange."

"Antonio!" his mother admonished.

"Well, it's true!" Antonio insisted.

"Don't worry, I think they're strange too," Feng said, giving the child an encouraging smile. He left the book on the tabletop in case Antonio changed his mind.

Their food and drinks arrived, but an uncomfortable wedge had emerged between them. Feng ate his peanut-butter bun with reverence, wondering why he'd waited so long to return to the café and eat them. He picked up his coffee cup, his hand accidentally knocking down the comic book. He bent to retrieve it, the movement toppling out a small box from his backpack that had been sitting on his lap.

"What are they?" Angie half-shrieked.

She pointed at the strange curved items in the clear box.

Feng smiled. "They're mangaka pens. These curved nibs are specially made for comic book art. You dip them in ink. Like this." He dug in his backpack for a bottle of ink, but Angie looked frightened.

"We have to go," she said.

"What's wrong?" Feng didn't understand.

Antonio looked at him. "She's scared of you. I know you didn't do it, Feng, but mom thinks they got the wrong guy."

Feng stared at him, his hand closing around the bottle in his backpack.

"Antonio!" Angie seemed unglued. She reached for her son. "Give him back his pencils!"

"No!" The boy seemed on the verge of tears. "They're mine. He gave them to me, right, Feng?"

Feng nodded. He felt shattered, but underneath it all, he understood Angie's anxiety. She'd been the victim of severe and sustained spousal abuse. She didn't trust men. Period.

"Angie," he said, reaching for the check which the waitress had slipped beside his plate. "I never hurt Mrs. Wei. The right man is in custody. He's even admitted his crime. I would never hurt you or Antonio. I know it's hard for you to trust me, or any man, but I was never anything but kind to you."

"I—"

Her protest died on her lips. Feng left a few extra dollars on the tip plate. He had to get out of here.

"Can I keep the comic book?" Antonio asked, clutching it like a shield.

"Sure," Feng said and left the café. Outside, the clouds swirled ominously. He didn't want to be here anymore.

And suddenly, he remembered. It was as if that golden god of a being stood right beside him, whispering to him.

Banpaia. Tenshi. Eternal love. Return to me.

CHAPTER THREE

Tenshi had to be very careful. Feng missed him. That much was obvious. He'd had no idea how sad and hurt Feng had been and he blamed himself for leaving him alone so long. Rules were rules however and once he'd broken them, there had been savage reprisals. Tenshi had been forced to wait a year, to see if he could live without Feng and vice versa.

He was certain Feng was starting to remember but the last thing he wanted was for Feng's precarious emotional state to shatter. He couldn't live with that. He followed him now as Feng walked down Hill Street back to the apartment. Tenshi was certain he saw Feng's shoulders drop a little. He didn't seem so hunched . . . so . . . defeated.

Feng walked with a renewed sense of purpose back to the apartment he shared with Russell. Tenshi hated seeing the bed the two men still shared, even if their sex life had been sporadic of late. He watched Feng drop his backpack onto a chair. Tenshi longed to touch the man's jaw. He missed Feng so much.

He watched as Feng fiddled with the computer keyboard and frowned. Feng's eyes filled with horror. Tenshi looked over his shoulder. Russell had accessed Feng's bank accounts. Feng quickly shut down the computer and ran to a closet, pulling out an old cigar box.

Tenshi could read Feng's mind. Russell had been through the contents.

"Oh, fuck," Feng said aloud. He took out all the papers, setting fire to everything in the kitchen sink. He put the empty cigar box back in the closet, throwing open windows to rid the room of the acrid smell.

Feng hid his backpack in a crevice between the bed and the wall. He lay down on the bed, passing a hand across his eyes.

Tenshi couldn't stand it. He lay beside the man he adored, watching a single tear leaking from the corner of his eye. He watched its slow progress toward Feng's ear.

"I'm here," Tenshi whispered. "I'm always here."

Feng resisted his tears. "Where are you?" he asked. "Are you here?"

Oh God . . . Feng wants me! He is ready!

Tenshi proceeded carefully. He captured the falling tear with his tongue, savoring the taste of Feng's heartache. Tenshi would make it all better. He would make it go away. With tentative, fluttering movements, he closed Feng's eyes.

"Remember," he said.

Feng let out a deep, wrenching howl when Tenshi returned him to the day he'd taken Feng to his special place, the field of ghost flowers. He'd carefully taken off all of Feng's clothes and laid his naked body on a carpet of the translucent white petals with their tiny red hearts.

He had sucked Feng's cock, licked his ass, then fucked him as Feng told him he could smell the flowers' petals.

Tenshi had driven deeply into his lover whose legs had wrapped themselves around Tenshi's hard thighs.

When he closed his eyes, Tenshi could remember it all. Few humans could smell the petals of the ghost flower. He knew Feng was the one for him because when he asked Feng what they smelled like, Feng inhaled deeply, his eyes looking dreamy and lust-filled at the same time.

"They smell like blood. They smell like . . . you."

Tenshi would have taken Feng right there and then, but the door to the apartment flew open. Russell came in, with Ki in tow. Feng sat up on the bed, struggling for composure.

"Hey, babe," Russell said, "Look who I found!"

"Ki!" Feng looked astonished.

"Hey," Ki said, snapping his fingers and pointing at Feng. "I remember you. I think."

Russell shrugged off his backpack and pulled out a sketch pad. He sat at the dining table, oblivious to Feng's red-rimmed eyes and the fact that he'd just brought home Ki, who for all intents and purposes had been missing for a year.

"Do I remember this place?" Ki asked, looking around.

"You should. You came here, I think." Russell looked confused now. "Did he come here, Feng?"

Feng nodded. "Where . . . how the . . . Ki, when did you get back?" Swinging his feet off the bed, Feng hastening over to him.

"Don't know. I think today. I saw Russell and followed him into the club and —"

"Crazy story," Russell said. "You don't want to hear it."

"Yes, I do," Feng said. "Go on, Ki."

"Next thing I know I'm on my knees sucking his cock."

"You what?" Feng asked, his eyes bulging in shock.

"Well, Vincent beat me to it, he was already sucking him, but then —"

"Oh, Christ," Russell said, dropping his pencil and covering his eyes.

"They both sucked you?" Feng seemed on the verge of collapse. He glanced at Russell's sketch book, a different expression coming over his eyes.

"That's him . . . it's him, Russell. You're drawing him! Have you seen him?"

"Er . . . no, not really. And er, what Ki just said, it's not what it sounds like," Russell started to say, but Feng's head had turned at the sound of thunder. He seemed excited now as he moved to the windows, where the red lanterns of Chinatown swung high in the air, casting a pale red glow over the inhabitants of the room.

Tenshi watched as Feng's face shone, Russell looked stricken and Ki looked confused.

Feng's emotions were so strong, yet oddly serene that Tenshi stood still.

"What is a ghost flower?" Feng suddenly asked.

"A what?" Ki asked.

Russell had picked up the sketch pad again. "Feng, are you okay?" He made a move toward Feng who stepped out of reach.

"Tea. I'd like some tea. How about you, Ki?"

"I don't know." Ki frowned. "I don't even know if I like tea."

"You always drank tea when I knew you," Feng said. He touched Ki's shoulder. "Come on. Let's leave the great artist to draw."

Russell watched his lover go off to the kitchen. He picked up his pencil, putting it down again. He fired up his laptop, glancing into the kitchen constantly.

He Googled ghost flower. *Fool.*

"Feng," he shouted, then stood up and walked into the kitchen. Feng and Ki seemed to be sharing a silent moment, waiting for the water to boil.

Tenshi watched from afar.

"I Googled ghost flowers and they bloom mostly in the desert."

"All year round?" Feng asked.

"Mostly around April, apparently."

Feng's facial expression changed. "Oh, I'm not waiting that long," he said.

"What?" Russell looked perplexed.

Feng brushed past him, retrieved his backpack, and walked into the kitchen.

"I hope you two will be very happy together. I have to wait 'til the flower blooms."

And with that, Feng walked out of the apartment with nothing but the clothes on his back and his backpack.

"That was weird." Ki gestured to the stove. "Water's boiling."

"No kidding." Russell turned off the pot. He would have run after Feng but frankly he had no idea what to say to him. Ki had blurted that they'd had sex. Feng took it well, on the whole. Until he'd started yapping about that stupid desert flower. What the hell did he mean he had to wait until it bloomed?

Ki was looking at him.

"What?" Russell asked.

"Are you going to make tea? I think I do want some now."

Russell wondered where Feng was going and why the apartment felt so chilly. When they'd all started disappearing, a strange, heavy fog had descended over the eastern part of the city. It had made the news, but the meteorologists couldn't agree on what it was. And then it went away.

For Russell, that heavy feeling had returned, an expectant, half scary feeling. The room felt weird, as if an unseen iceberg had dropped into the middle of it. He reached out a hand as if he might be able to touch it then shook his head. Nah. He was just a little freaked because Feng had walked out. He made tea, not really worried about Feng. He was probably walking. He'd come back. His box full of papers was still here, not to mention his clothes.

"What's happening?" Ki asked as he sipped his tea. "I feel as if I'm not really here."

"It will pass."

"What do you remember?"

"I remember," Russell closed his eyes, "pleasure."

Ki put down his tea. "I want to feel that again." He stood, looked at Russell. "Now."

Feng wasn't sure where he was going but he was pretty confident he'd end up in the right place. He was thinking about those ghost flowers. They grew in Southern California and in Arizona and Nevada. They were mainly translucent white but flecked with red, the leaves hairy and slender, growing upwards to the sky. The plant was small, growing in clumps in rocky slopes and dry washes.

He could see them now as he walked. Purity and blood. Hearty and territorial, they needed little nurturing to exist. *My love. Take me. Take me back to your embrace. I made a mistake. I'm willing to give you everything.*

A single tear rolled down Feng's cheek. He kept walking, the backpack weighing heavy on his back. The people and buildings whirled by him. He didn't see them anymore. They whizzed by faster and faster and then Feng froze. He looked around. No traffic. No people. Only hot, dry air surrounded him. Sand and rocks. And Ghost flowers.

Ki took off Russell's shirt and licked his chest. At the same time, he undid his pants and roughly fondled Russell's erection. Russell's guilt at cheating on Feng was slowing disappearing. Feng had left him already. He was looking for something Russell feared he'd never find.

The face in front of him was filled with beauty. Hands pushed him to the floor and touched him everywhere. Russell closed his eyes. *It's you. Stay with me.*

Don't speak.

Ki's face loomed over his as he drove his fingers up inside of Russell's ass. He didn't even remember being naked. *Pleasure.* He cried out something unintelligible and strong hands flipped him onto his stomach.

Two voices now discussed him as if he wasn't in the room. *You lick him there and I'll fondle his genitals. I get to have him first. No. Me. You can have me, Vincent!*

Vincent? Russell tried to turn over but there was a tongue doing a sensual dance around his anus, and a hand squeezing his already tightening balls. *How in hell did Vincent get here? Pleasure!*

Russell cried out as fingers fucked him and then a cock stabbed him a few times before spreading his thighs and driving up hard inside him. He howled out, pain and pleasure mingling in a delicious harmony. *It's over. You and Feng. You can have them both. I give them to you. Your sex slaves. Or choose.*

One, then the other, took him, fucking him hard and deep. Then he was dragged up to his knees. He found himself looking into Vincent's eyes. Vincent kissed him while stroking his cock which was on the way up again. The body behind him pulled out then sliced back in. Russell shuddered, every nerve excited. Vincent twisted his nipples and stroked his cock some more. Russell's head went back.

"Oh no," Vincent licked his lips, taking his own cock in hand. "I need some attention. Ki, push the boy forward."

Vincent lay down on his back and pulled Russell's face forward. "Suck it," he urged as Ki kept pounding his ass from behind.

Russell moaned as he began to play with Vincent's big erection then he licked the head. Ki pushed his head down further to Vincent's cock and Russell took it into his mouth.

Ki came inside Russell then pulled out. He replaced his cock with three fingers and moved them around. Russell moved his hips, in sync with Ki's probing fingers, and took Vincent's cock deeper into his throat. *Um. Now this was hot!*

Tenshi watched Feng as he stood in the middle of the barren space. He should have been confused, agitated. Instead

Tenshi sensed that his heart was filled with hope and it pleased him. It was time, time to go and meet him, to flood all those memories back to his mind and his heart.

Wait.

Tenshi swallowed hard. It was what he was dreading. *Can't we make an exception?*

You failed to capture his heart. You sent the other away although his heart had already promised to you. I have punished you for that. If you pursue this, you will warrant the ultimate punishment.

Tenshi's gaze settled on Feng.

You have been bestowed everything that was mine and yet you mock it.

No. I . . . would never be so callous.

Make your choice, Tenshi, but make sure you are fully aware of what that will mean . . . to both of you.

It was gone. The voice. That's all it was, a voice which once belonged to his master. When the master had lost the will to go on, he chose the one to take his place. Resurrected from their privileged resting places, the master chose two for the final contest. The victor then took his place. However, the master's voice had power, and could punish if one of the commandments were broken.

His powers had already been diminished because Feng had rejected him, and he had ultimately sent Vincent back to his life. Out of guilt, he made sure Vincent would be successful in whatever he chose to do with his life. The master didn't appreciate this gesture.

He could leave here now, restore Feng's life, his love affair with Russell, and wander the Earth looking for the next candidate. Or . . . Or he could pay the ultimate price in exchange for being in Feng's arms for the next say . . . sixty years?

"Tenshi!"

Feng's voice rang out plaintively.

"Don't leave me here alone!"

He couldn't give him the gift. He'd have none to give. If Feng came to him now, he'd come for only him, and him alone.

"Tenshi!"

"I'm here."

Feng turned his head in Feng's direction. His gaze settled on him as Feng moved forward. Tears welled up in his eyes. "I left you." He dropped to his knees as Tenshi approached. He looked up. "I'm sorry. I want to come back. Please. My life is meaningless without you."

Tenshi placed a hand on Feng's head for a second then removed it. "Please, rise."

Feng stumbled to his feet.

Tenshi smiled tenderly at him. "Everything is different now."

"You don't want me anymore?"

"No, the problem is, I do want you."

Feng wrapped his arms around his neck and held onto him. Tenshi felt himself weaken even more. *What will I do as a mortal man? I wouldn't know how to live that way.* Tenshi disentangled himself from Feng. "Walk with me."

Feng looked at him curiously. "All right."

They walked for a while, their feet shifting through sand. There seemed to be no air, but Feng didn't mind it. His mind was a jumbled mess of memory and sensation. He only knew that the being that walked with him had offered his heart and for some reason, he'd rejected him. "You're not human," he said suddenly.

"You know what I am." He turned and met his gaze.

Feng nodded. "Blood drinker." He said the words almost reverently and as he did, the skies went dark. Only the stars now led them. "I want to stay with you always. I love you."

He smiled. "And I love you."

Those words brought joy to Feng's heart. "Where are we going?"

"I don't know," he stopped and looked up at the sky. "He is awakening. I feel it. His wrath will know no bounds."

Feng's eyes widened. "Who?"

"The master."

"But you have no master."

"I did once. The chains will again tighten."

"He hurt you?"

"He controlled me."

"Did you give him your heart?"

Tenshi had to think about that. It was so very long ago. "I did in the beginning. He was too beautiful. The pleasure he gave too intense. Addictive."

"What happened?"

"My time with him passed and I went to my rest. When he grew tired, he brought me back, me and Shuguy."

"Shuguy," Feng tasted the word on his mouth. "Shuguy." Something about that name made him draw his breath. A battle. He saw a battle. "You destroyed him." Feng looked at him. "Did you love him?"

Tenshi took a few steps back as if Feng had suddenly struck him.

"He loved you, too, but the love could never be. The master hated that he loved you. He wanted both of you to love him, and him alone. You wept as you took his head."

"How . . . how do you know this?" Tenshi gasped.

Feng came closer. He reached out and touched Tenshi's face. "Don't you recognize me, my love?"

Something was happening to Vincent. His face was contorted, not with orgasm, but with something else. He began to thrash as if he was having convulsions. Russell and Ki stood over him helplessly as Vincent started to scream out words in an ancient language neither man had ever heard before.

"What's he saying?" Ki asked.

"I have no idea," Russell shook his head.

"Should we call an ambulance?"

Russell nodded and raced to the phone. While he was giving directions on the phone, Ki was calling to him. Russell came running with the receiver. "He's stopped breathing," Ki looked up at Russell. "What do we do?"

Russell's jaw fell. "Shit, I . . . well . . . he's stopped breathing," he said into the phone.

The woman on the other line told him to calm down. "I'm going to tell you what to do," she said. "Ambulance is on its way."

Russell and Ki followed every instruction, breathing into Vincent's mouth and pressing on his chest. They were still doing it when the two medics arrived. They took over for a while, but they didn't seem optimistic.

Ki and Russell stood in the corner of the room, distraught. The medics loaded a lifeless Vincent onto a stretcher and took him outside. "Should we go with them?" Ki asked.

Russell nodded. "I guess we'll have to. There'll be questions. He's naked, too. They'll going to know he had sex."

"They're not going to think we killed him, are they?" Ki chewed his thumb nail.

"Think he had a heart attack?" Russell asked. Even as he said it, it didn't make sense. Vincent had been mumbling some strange language. It sounded Asian but Russell couldn't understand a word. It wasn't Japanese. It wasn't Chinese or Korean either.

"Could have," Ki replied.

Russell forgot what he'd said before. "What?"

"He could have had a heart attack from all the sex. Nice way to go."

Russell made a face. "He was too young to die."

Ki nodded. "Yes, I know. We better go."

Russell locked the door and followed Ki outside to his car. He would have liked to have told Feng, but he didn't know where he'd gone or if he'd even care.

Ki paid the exorbitant parking fee at the hospital. They entered emergency. The two medics stood there at the desk. One of them had his head in his hands. Had he known Vincent? He seemed to be taking it really hard.

The other medic suddenly looked in their direction. He made a beeline for them and he looked pissed off. Russell was horrified when the man grabbed Ki by the front of his shirt and shook him. "Is this your idea of a sick fucking joke? How did you do it? How in hell did you do it?"

Everyone was staring. Ki was speechless and Russell tried to drag the medic off him. "We didn't do anything. What are you talking about?" Russell shouted.

The medic turned his attention on Russell. "What am I talking about? I'm talking about how you managed to get that guy we brought in to play dead?"

"Play dead?" Ki managed, looking at Russell.

"Yeah," the medic grunted. "When we got him here to emergency, we opened the back of the bus and he just walked out."

Russell's eyes widened. "No shit."

"No shit," the medic replied as the hospital security guard walked up to them.

"What's going on?" She said, looking at everyone.

"Call the police," the other medic came up to them now. "These two clowns got a lot to answer for."

42

Chapter Four

The touch of his hand sent Tenshi back in time. It seemed like yesterday that he wandered the stone walls of the monastery hidden away deep in the mountains. With only the torchlight to guide him, he longed for a time when he would be delivered, and he could see in the darkness, like *him*. They all loved him, all longed for his favor, the touch of his hand. The privileged few that had been given access to the inner sanctum, his own private chambers where Tenshi knew one was transformed.

He'd never dared dream that maybe one day that, *he*, the master, the Lord whose name could not be murmured aloud, would choose him as his beloved. Only ten of them had been selected, brought here to dwell with him in this hidden paradise. Their time was spent praising him, paying homage to his power and beauty, training hard to be a strong warrior, a noble, disciplined follower of a god of which the world had never seen.

As a young man, Tenshi found the sexual restrictions the hardest. If his cock was hard when he awoke in the morning, he had to confess and receive punishment. The master would watch from a coveted place where one of his disciples would strip him and bind his cock. He'd be taken to a public place where all could watch, his wrists tied above his head while his cock would be gently whipped into submission. The blood would be collected and taken to the master, as a sacrifice to him. Tenshi saw himself now, his head back, wincing in pain as the whip struck his sex.

He was sure that the master would never choose him. His sins against the flesh were frequent, no matter how pure he tried to keep his thoughts. And then just when Tenshi thought he was mastering his sexual desires, Shuguy. Shuguy was the closest thing he'd ever seen to the devil. Not because he had an evil bone in his body. He was actually sweet and kind, with great patience and inner strength. But his beauty and sensuality were more than Tenshi could stand.

There he was, standing in front of him as Tenshi tried to navigate through the dimly lit corridors of the hallowed halls. They came face to face and Tenshi told his cock to behave.

"You avoid me," he accused, standing in Tenshi's path. "Have I done something to offend?"

Tenshi licked his lips. He looked at anything except his face. "I ah . . ." he studied the cold stone floor, focused on the scratching of a rodent somewhere close by. "You have done nothing. I am . . . busy."

Shuguy met his gaze. "Would you take a walk with me later?"

"No." He shook his head and brushed by.

Shuguy reached out and grabbed his arm. Tenshi felt his touch to the bone. "Please, Tenshi. We can meditate together outside near the wall."

Tenshi looked at him. The last thing he wanted to do with Shuguy was to meditate. "I don't think so. We shouldn't be alone together," he shook loose and hurried on his way.

All that day, he tried to concentrate on his studies, but his mind would stray to Shuguy. His smile, his voice and ultimately, Tenshi would image them together, their scratchy robes discarded, skin touching skin. At the end of the day, his cock was hard again. He punished himself by skipping supper and going to his room early. He didn't confess his wayward thoughts or the result.

As the days and nights passed, he was consumed by erotic

dreams of Shuguy, dreams which tempted him to touch himself, although he didn't dare actually give himself any relief. He thought he could deceive the master. He was wrong.

At the end of a long day, precisely a month after Shuguy had arrived, he was summoned to the room he knew so well, where he'd been often punished for allowing his sex to stiffen with desire.

He was confused as he accompanied one of the disciples. "What have I done?" His question was ignored.

He was led to the center of the room where the chains and manacles lay. The disciple left him. He looked around the cold room, thinking he was alone. The torches flickered in the wind and went out. Tenshi sucked in some breath. He heard *his* voice. He said his name. *Tenshi.* It was like music, lyrical and seductive. "Master," he fell to his knees, lowered his head to the cold floor.

"Rise!"

Tenshi got to his feet, peering through the blackness, longing for a glimpse of him.

"You have been a very bad boy, Tenshi."

Tenshi stiffened.

"Every night you dream of him."

"Master, I . . . forgive me." He knew. He knew his very thoughts.

"It is forbidden. You must remain pure if you are to be chosen."

"Yes, master. I am pure . . . in body."

"If your mind is impure then so are you." There was anger in his voice. "Remove your robe!"

Tenshi pulled his robe over his head.

"Hands out to your sides."

Slowly he extended his arms.

"You dream of impaling him with your organ. You dreamt of yanking back his head and burying your organ deep in his throat. Touch yourself!"

"Master, it is forbidden. I . . ."

"I command you!"

Shamed faced, Tenshi began to stroke his organ. It hardened in his fist.

"Close your eyes, lick your lips. Use your other hand to caress your nakedness. Naked, and ashamed. Dirty, dirty boy. Harder, faster. Stroke it!"

Tenshi was lost to his voice. He moaned with pleasure at each jerking motion, pinching his nipples, handling his testicles until he let out a cry and the cream flowed through his fingers.

"Hands high in the air!"

Tenshi lifted up his arms. He gasped as the chains lifted from the floor and clasped his wrists.

In the darkness that surrounded him he felt movement and suddenly hands fondling his cock, bringing it again to the state of erection. Hands cupped his buttocks, separated, and explored his deepest most intimate cavity. Undiscovered pleasures lay there, and tongues brought them to the surface. Someone knelt at his feet and took his organ deep in their mouths. A hard cock sliced his buttocks wide and spread him open where hard, thick organs played and teased. Completely filled and handled, his orgasms came hard and fast, one after another until he could hardly stand the pleasure. "Please."

"Is this what you want to do to Shuguy?" The voice spoke near his ear. "Confess." Fingers played with his nipples, pulled, and tongued and flicked them.

"Yessss."

"Tell me."

A hand was again playing with his cock. "I want to fill his . . . his ass with my . . . I want to dominate him and use his ass for my pleasure."

Teeth nibbled his neck. "You shall have him but only when

46

I say. Under my eye. Do you understand?"

"Yes."

"Take him without me and I'll kill you."

Tenshi howled in pain as two needle sharp teeth bit deep into his throat. He heard the gulping and swallowing as hands played with his body. His eyes closed.

When they opened again, he was still hanging there. Dried blood caked his chest. The torches were lit, and he blinked. Was he to die here?

When he heard footsteps, he looked up. "Shuguy?"

Shuguy's eyes widened. He ran to him. "Are you alive?"

He smiled. "Yes. I wouldn't be talking to you if I wasn't."

Shuguy ran his gaze over him then blushed. "You are very beautiful."

"You should look away."

"I cannot."

"What are you doing here?"

"I was sent here."

"Why?"

The torches flickered.

"I don't know."

"Touch him," a voice commanded.

"Who . . . who . . . was that?" He looked at Tenshi. "Is it him?"

"Yes," Tenshi said. He closed his eyes. He knew what pleasures he could share with Shuguy now. It was worse since he had tasted the forbidden fruit.

"Touch him!" That voice bellowed, shaking the very walls around them.

"Do it," Tenshi said. "He'll kill you."

Shuguy's eyes changed. They became red and brilliant. He placed his hands on Tenshi's chest and began to lick the dry blood while he fondled Tenshi's balls. When he reached under and began to tease his hole, Tenshi couldn't believe it.

Shuguy glanced up at him, his eyes boldly looking into his. His voice was like music when he announced, "I'm going to possess your ass, Tenshi, then I'm going to take your soul."

Russell sat tensely behind Ki in the interrogation room while a huge, gruff lieutenant declared that he planned to make their lives a living hell until they 'came clean' about what had happened to the dead guy.

"There's nothing to come *clean about*," Russell said for the third time.

"Yeah man, we're as confused as you are," Ki added.

Lieutenant Staples put his foot up on the chair and combed his graying hair with his thick, calloused fingers. "Look, I got all night. I would prefer to be home sleeping next to the little woman but hey . . . life sucks. Corpses don't get up and walk away. I know there's a way to temporarily stop the heart. The medics say the guy was dead. I believe it. So, all I can come up with is that this is some kind of a scam." He pointed at them. "And you two are in it up to your necks."

The lieutenant took out a pack of smokes and slid them over to Russell and Ki. Russell didn't smoke, but it there was any time to take it up, it was now. He grabbed the pack and stuck one in his mouth. The Lieutenant reached over and lit it with his lighter.

Ki stared at him and waved his hand in front of his face, coughing. Russell took a few deep drags and began hacking himself, deciding to stub it out in the tobacco can lid sitting in the middle for that purpose.

"Now, start over," the cop said. He had piercing watery blue eyes, overshadowed by heavy drooping lids and thick eyebrow which cried out for a trim. He meant business.

"We told you," Ki said. "We were . . . ah . . . fooling around and . . ."

"Fucking. You were fucking and?"

"Yeah," Russell nodded. "No law against it."

"Nope. Probably should be. Go on."

"He just stopped breathing," Russell sighed.

"We did mouth to mouth," Ki said, "called the ambulance. You must have it on record."

"Then what happened?"

"They told us to keep doing the CPR," Russell said. "We did, taking turns, but he didn't respond. The medics got there say . . . ten minutes later. They took over for a while then told us he was dead. That's it."

"After that," Ki threw up his hands, "we followed the ambulance to the hospital and when we arrived, the medic attacked us, saying that Vincent got up and walked away. We know nothing about that, officer. I swear."

"We got an APB on him." Stapleton stood. "You guys are being held until we find him and get some answers."

"You're holding us on what?" Russell demanded.

"Suspicion."

"Suspicion of doing what?" Ki protested. "I know my rights. I want a lawyer."

"You get one phone call," he said, motioning to the guard. "Take care of these clowns."

Russell stared at Ki. Ki placed a hand on his shoulder. "Don't worry, we'll call Joby."

Tenshi was aware that Shuguy was not quite himself. The timid and beautiful young man of his fantasies had become a needy, sexual animal. *Tenshi. Say my name.*

Hands moved over his flesh. It felt as if he was being swallowed whole. *Say my name.*

Kenshen.

The name floated in Tenshi's head. The all-knowing, the

eternal. Penetrated, taken, possessed.

"You are mine!"

He was on his knees, the chains broken and Shuguy, strong and powerful used his body while voices whispered about their lust. His entire body trembled as he was spread and impaled. His eyes rolled back in his head. "Say. My. Name."

"Kenshen! Kenshen!" He cried, collapsing on the frigid stone. Hands came to drag him across the floor and darkness deepened around him, lulling him off to a place where white flowers blossomed. He sighed as he lay in a field of white petals. Then drops, tiny drops of blood fell from the sky, painting the petals with flecks of red. *Ghost Flower. They are for you, my beauty. Forever yours.*

The following morning Tenshi awoke in his bed, feeling stiff and used. He rose before the sunlight as usual and ate his meager breakfast of freshly baked bread and oat cereal. He looked across the table at Shuguy but there didn't seem to be any acknowledgement of what had transpired between them. *Kenshen.* Was he to be the chosen, the one *he* took to be at his side for the next two hundred years? He wondered.

The others regarded him suspiciously now. Perhaps they knew of the special attention he was receiving from him. He knew his name now, and he wanted to sing it at the top of his voice, but it was forbidden.

As soon as breakfast was over, Tenshi meditated. On his knees, head pressed to the floor he asked for salvation and for favor. When the bell tinkled in his ear, he rose and went to the library where he was in the process of painstakingly transcribing the ancient scripts. Tibetan was written in a very conservative syllabify script based on the writing system of the ancient Sanskrit language of India. One needed not only to be a scholar but also an artist. The finest of calligraphy was used as presentation.

Tenshi was in the process of concentrating on his task, head bent over a candlelit page of parchment when a voice said his name. He looked up to see Shuguy standing there. How beautiful he was. He could almost abandon his desire to dwell with *him,* in exchange for Shuguy in his bed.

"Will you walk with me this evening?"

"Yes," he said. "I will walk with you."

Shuguy smiled, nodding his head. "I will return to my chores."

That evening, Tenshi sat silently, sipping his broth with his brothers, but inside, he was anxious, anxious to spend some time alone with Shuguy. Perhaps they could walk near the wall, look out over the beautiful water. In the mountains, they seemed so close to the sky. The stars were beautiful when the sun went down.

Shuguy was the first to take his bowl and leave the table. Tenshi waited until he could wait no more and followed.

Outside, Shuguy washed his bowl in the barrel filled with water. He looked up as Tenshi approached but didn't say anything. He waited while Tenshi washed his own dish and set it aside.

It was already dark, those stars brilliantly winking at them from above. Tenshi began to walk. Shuguy fell in step beside him. They didn't speak until they reached the wall. They were both out of breath. The terrain was rocky and uneven. *Did he remember? Did Shuguy remember touching him, being inside of him, or had Kenshen stripped him of all memory?*

Tenshi rested his hands on the wall. He surveyed the dark earth around him. Shuguy's hand slid over his. Tenshi turned and looked at him. "I love you," Shuguy whispered.

Tenshi stifled a moan. "And I, you."

Their gazes met.

"Kiss me," Tenshi urged.

Shuguy displayed that same shyness he always had. It was really him. Shuguy lifted a hand and touched Tenshi's cheek. He moved closer, reaching up, he touched his mouth to his.

Tenshi slipped his arm around Shuguy's waist and pulled him closer. Shuguy groaned, his hands moving over Tenshi's stiff garb. "I need you," he whispered. "Although it's wrong, it's all I think about."

Tenshi moved his lips to Shuguy's neck. He kissed him there, speaking in his ear. "It's not wrong. It can't be. It is too beautiful. You fill my dreams. You fill my heart."

"Fill me," Shuguy urged. "Please. Take me. Here. Now. If I am to be punished, let it be."

Tenshi roughly positioned Shuguy facing the wall. He yanked up his robe to find his beautiful creamy naked ass. He massaged his globes, slapped it a few times then reached between his legs to stroke his cock, which was as hard as his own. One hand on Shuguy's head, he nudged his thighs further apart, and used some of his own juices which were now coating the head of his cock, to loosen Shuguy's entrance.

A coated finger, then two, played up inside Shuguy, who wiggled his intoxicating buttocks, increasing Tenshi's urgency to be inside of him. He played some more there, stroking Shuguy's cock over and over to ready him. With his own robe around his waist, Tenshi positioned the head of his aching cock between Shuguy's delectable butt cheeks and pushed up inside of him.

His hand moved over Shuguy's mouth to stifle his cries as he thrust harder and harder, delving deeper as he bent him further over the wall. As their passion intensified, it became more difficult to contain their joy. Neither one of them heard the approaching footsteps but abruptly Tenshi was ripped away from his lover, and both of them taken to that room, to await judgment.

Russell was surprised to see Joby, the man he'd witnessed dressed in drag, show up dressed in a dark-blue tailored suit, carrying a briefcase. He was as beautiful a man, as he was a woman.

He shook hands with Ki and Russell and laid his briefcase on the table. "I'm sorry I wasn't able to come until this morning."

Russell shrugged. "I doubt they would have let us go anyway." He couldn't stop looking at him. He had jet black hair, a little curly, with big green eyes, and was taller than he thought. He could have easily passed for Caucasian.

"I've been briefed on the charges against you. Can you explain to me in your own words what happened?"

Ki began to talk, telling him the details and Russell was trying to remember where he'd seen him before. Had he too been taken by Tenshi? Perhaps not. Maybe he'd encountered him in the neighborhood. Ki seemed to know. Russell thought he wouldn't mind encountering him in bed. *Yum.* Obviously, he worked out. He could see the body definition under that suit.

"Russell?"

Ki was speaking to him. He shook himself. "Yeah?"

"Did you have anything to add?" Joby asked, jotting down a few notes.

Russell shook his head.

"I'll see if I can get bail arranged," Joby stood, snapping his briefcase shut.

"How much we talking?" Russell asked him.

"You have no money?" Joby looked at him.

Russell shook his head. If only he could reach Feng. Feng would lend him the money.

"I don't mind helping you guys out," he said, "but if you can't make bail . . . we're talking at least a few thousand, then . . ." He shrugged. "I'm sorry."

"Damn it."

"There are bail bondsmen," he suggested, looking genuinely concerned.

"They break your legs if you don't pay, right?" Ki muttered.

He laughed. "Not the legit ones. Look, I'll see what I can do. I don't quite understand about this Vincent guy. I'll try to do some research, find out more about him."

"We told you all we know. He has money and he's an actor," Ki offered.

"It could be a publicity stunt but . . ." Joby placed a hand on the door jam, "seems pretty lame."

Russell nodded.

"I'll get back to you as soon as I can," he said. "Try not to panic."

He was gone. Panic. They were both way beyond panic. "Publicity stunt?" Ki shook his head. "Why would Vincent do this to us?"

"There's more to this than that," Russell said. He'd been thinking all night in that stinking cell. "What if Tenshi took him back?"

"Tenshi can do that?" Ki's eyes widened.

"He can do anything."

"Then we're screwed. Who's going to believe us?"

Russell couldn't disagree. The entire mess was just too much. After the guard came and took them back to their cell, Russell asked Ki the question he'd been dying to ask all along. "Where do we know him from?"

"Who, Joby Hayes?"

"Is that his name?"

"Um, father was English or something."

"Yeah, so where do we know him from?"

"The club. He works there one night a week, doing drag. He came over to talk to you one night, asked to buy you a drink. You turned him down."

"Was I nuts?"

Ki laughed. "You've always been nuts, Russell."

Russell snarled at him.

"Don't worry. Joby will find a way. He's a good lawyer."

"We have no way to pay him."

Ki winked. "I'm sure you'll come up with something."

CHAPTER FIVE

Tenshi and Shuguy stood naked in that room, the torches blazing menacingly around them. They stood there for what seemed forever until the door opened and seven of their brothers walked in.

One, a tall gaunt brother, called Tanasak, wielded a whip in his hand. He nodded at the others, who immediately grabbed Tenshi and Shuguy and shackled their hands over their heads.

"Legs spread," Tanasak shouted. "Dirty, dirty, boys." He looked at one of the youngest two brothers, as he slapped the whip in his hand. "You will stroke them to hardness."

The two brothers immediately obeyed, fondling, and stroking them until their cocks were erect. Immediately, the whip came down on one erect cock then the other. Tenshi and Shuguy cried out.

"Silence!" Their torturer commanded. He nodded again to the brothers who moved around behind them. Tenshi felt himself being opened as a warm stiff object moved up inside of him. Each time the whip hit his erect penis, the brother behind him moved the object in and out. The whip moved from his cock to his chest until he felt he would lose consciousness.

Shuguy had already passed out beside him.

Every time, Tenshi's cock softened, brothers came to stiffen it. As time passed, the eyes that gazed at him filled with lust, the smiles became leers as he was played with, the object replaced with their organs. It was as if they were possessed, pleasure derived by the pain of that whip. Darkness eventually overcame him. It was worth it. *He would remember Shuguy forever.*

When Tenshi opened his eyes, it was to darkness. He tried to move his body, but he was confined. He began to scream, palms pushing upwards. He was in a coffin.

This modern world was like nothing he'd ever seen. People everywhere, flashing lights and materials which seemed artificial. Who controlled this world? Who made the rules?

He'd looked everywhere for the ghost flower. There were flowers of the likes he'd never seen before carefully positioned around sculptured pieces of grass, but no pure petals flecked with blood.

It was so strange, he thought, as he continued walking. Mortals in this time had somehow tried to master nature itself, everything conveniently arranged in their own image. On every corner, prepared food, and items which seemed completely useless for survival. There were little and big cube things which actually carried them from place to place, as if they all were royalty. And there was no unison among them, nothing to identify them by tribe or rank, a mash of people, hurrying off in various directions, coming in and out of doors. And the smell, it smelled bad. The sky filled with ugly patches and streams of poison floated up into the universe. What had they done to their world?

It was an affront against everything sacred. The smells and sights were making his head spin. He was hungry. Time to feed. So many morsels to choose from. He stood on the corner, watching a strange light change color. People stood still or moved based on what color the light was. Perhaps here was their god. The god of light. Even the little cubes carrying the mortals obeyed. Perhaps the mortals in the cubes were gods. The smaller gods in smaller cubes, and they controlled the lights.

He looked around him. He spotted a young man

approaching. He stood beside him, watching that light intently. He seemed impatient.

He snaked out a hand and closed his fingers around his wrist, bringing him close. His prey was unable to speak. He smiled at him. He could taste the blood.

Say my name.

Kenshen.

Tenshi's cries had gone in vain. He scratched the top of the coffin until his fingers ran with blood. He was alive and yet . . . what was he? Was he dead? Was he sleeping? It was a long time before Kenshen chose to answer.

The silence was almost too much to bear, the darkness paralyzing. *Please.*

You may plead all you want. It isn't time yet.

So grateful to hear another voice, even if it was in his head, Tenshi began to weep. "Kenshen. Please," he whispered.

"You love him more than me."

"No."

"Don't lie to me. I know your heart. You snuck away with him to the wall, pounded his sweet little ass. You did not think of me once."

"You are jealous and vindictive!" Tenshi didn't think before he spoke. He felt a stabbing pain to his heart.

"How dare you! You survive because I will it."

Tenshi winced from the pain. "Kill me then. Anything is better than this."

"The time is coming when I must take another. You were my first choice. Not anymore."

"I don't care. Finish this!"

"Oh, I will, or you will."

The voice sounded sinister now. Pure evil. Why hadn't he realized it before?

"What does that mean?" Silence closed around him again. "Kenshen! Come back! Don't leave me! Please. Come back!"

"What do you mean exactly?" Joby lifted an eyebrow.

Ki cleared his throat. Russell didn't think it was a good idea to tell Joby about their supernatural experiences, but Ki insisted that Joby would understand.

Twenty-four hours almost in jail, with no sight of Vincent, and no hope of parole.

"Ki, don't," Russell said.

"Listen," Joby said, "if I'm going to help you, you got to tell me the truth."

"You won't believe us," Russell sighed.

"Try me," he smiled.

Oh, he'd love to try him, anytime, baby. He shook himself. "Ever heard of Banpaia?"

"In comic books."

"For real," Russell met those beautiful green eyes.

"Go on." He sat back in the seat.

"He comes every two hundred years to choose a mate. We think he took possession of Vincent's body."

"Why would he do that? He has his own body."

Ki looked at Russell. "See! He believes us."

Russell wasn't looking at Ki. He was looking right at Joby. "You know him."

He stood up. "Tenshi didn't possess your friend's body. He'd have no use for it. He is far more beautiful anyway. Whatever did," he lowered his voice, "is far more sinister than Tenshi. All I can say is, God save us."

Russell and Ki were staring at him.

"I've got to get you both out of here before he comes for you," Joby picked up his briefcase. "I'll put up the bail money myself."

Someone had deceived him, and that deception had taken place hundreds of years ago. *Tenshi.* How did he do it? They would feel his wrath, both of them. *You won't have my Tenshi, Shuguy.*

He dropped the startled mortal in the street, feeling re-freshed, strong, as those strange mortals screamed around him. Some high-pitched sound assaulted his ears and he placed his hands over them and kept on walking, ignoring the light god. "You're not my god!" he yelled as those little cubes made funny noises and came to a dead halt around him. He rose into the air as funny little metal things flew at him. He reached out and caught them in his fist. They were hot. He threw them back, rising higher as more screeching sounds ap-proached.

Where are you, Tenshi? Where are the flowers I made in your honor, my love? I'm coming and I will destroy you but all in good time.

He relished a bit of play first. Flying high he scanned the ground below. The landscape changed. There were less peo-ple and very few shelters made of odd materials. There was only sand and rock . . . and . . . yes, he smiled, ghost flowers.

As he floated in the sky, which was gradually fading to night, he remembered touching Tenshi. Ah, the pleasure of tasting him, drinking from him, and the joy in knowing that he was his. It didn't matter that deep down Tenshi despised him. He didn't care about that. He owned him, body and soul.

His thoughts went back to that night when he'd released both Tenshi and Shuguy from their death boxes. They were badly shaken, distraught and oh so happy to see one another. He'd chained them naked to opposite sides of the wall, made them watch as possessed brothers had their way with them. Then, he made his grand appearance.

He dispensed of all the others and floated down to the cen-ter of the room, dressed in his finest attire. They were in awe of him, daunted by his beauty, at the same time terrified and fascinated. He loved the expression on their faces. He went to Tenshi first, his obsession, though he would never tell him that. He ran his fingers over his fine chest, lifted his sex in his hand. "You are mine."

Tenshi lowered his head.

He'd looked at the other, stood aside to show him how he held Tenshi's sex in his hand. "Mine."

Shuguy looked stricken for a moment then quite clearly, he said, "No."

Tenshi lifted his head at that moment, looking at Shuguy and it was then Kenshen made his decision. He released Tenshi and walked to the center of the room. "Tonight, you will fight one another to the death. The survivor will become mine for the next two hundred years."

When Kenshen left them, they were crying bitter tears. Kenshen knew it was the worse fate he could bestow upon them. And although he was sure that Tenshi would be the victor, he wasn't going to take any chances because his heart would break if he lost his beloved.

He ordered that Shuguy be taken from the room and beaten, making sure to leave bleeding wounds on his body. Then he went to Tenshi, who still hung naked in the room.

As he approached, he let the robe he wore drop to the floor. He showed his true self, the needle-sharp fangs and the blood-red eyes. His nails grew sharp and long, and he almost slithered to his naked prize. He raked his nails down the center of Tenshi's chest, and Tenshi brought forth a cry. Kenshen licked the droplets of blood as they rose to the surface all the way to Tenshi's beautiful sex.

"Hard," he whispered. "You will stand hard and proud for me, my love."

Tenshi's cock stiffened and grew. Tenshi let out a cry.

"I can make you do anything," he whispered. "Thick," he

licked his red lips. "You are thick and hard. So beautiful, you make angels cry . . . because you are an angel. I stole you from the heavens itself. Did you know?"

Tenshi shook his head.

Kenshen touched his erection quite casually, tormenting it, making it ache and ooze. He walked around him, running his hands down Tenshi's back, separating his ass cheeks and inserting his hot and wild tongue which he extended until it went deep inside Tenshi.

Tenshi twisted and begged but the more he did, the more Kenshen slithered his tongue inside him, reaching around to slap and cuff his erection. "You feel so good," he grunted after he withdrew his tongue. He came around to the front again. He licked each nipple, bit into them, all the while fondling his sex, cupping his ballsack, never giving him relief.

"I will give you my gift. Tonight, you will thirst, and you will drink him dry. I want," he came close, opening his jaws, his sharp teeth glistening, "I want you to fuck him before you drain him. Is that clear?" He bent to sink his teeth deep into Tenshi's throat. In ecstasy he drank from his angel, the nectar of his blood sacred and pure, like the flowers. One day he'd have to pay for his theft but not yet. He drank and he drank until Tenshi neared the end. "You won't die. You can't. You're immortal like me." He smiled, touching his body at his leisure before transforming him. "Angel of death," he whispered. "That's what you are now." He reached up and undid the chains.

Tenshi fell at his feet. Kenshen fed him his cock. "Suck and drink. Tonight, you will do my bidding, my beauty, and then I will possess you for my own."

Russell and Ki relaxed at Joby's condo. It was amazing how quickly he'd gotten them out of jail. The news was filled with the appearance of a mysterious man who apparently had drunk someone's blood and dodged bullets in the sky.

"Would Tenshi do that?" Ki wrinkled his nose.

Russell shook his head. "No." He checked his cell phone. "No word at all from Feng. I've left him several messages. He must have seen the news."

"I'm scared. Who do you think possessed poor Vincent?"

"You're half in love with him," Russell accused. "I though you have a thing for me?" He was grinning.

"You don't seem so upset," Ki threw back from where he was laying on the sofa.

"That Joby is a mystery," Russell smiled.

"You got the hots for him."

"You bet."

Ki made a face. "So, I guess we won't be a thing."

"Naw."

"What about Feng?"

"He loves Tenshi."

"We all love him. Doesn't mean I'd move in with him."

"It's more than that." Russell walked over to the window. "Way more."

When the door opened, Russell turned around and Ki jumped off the sofa. Joby stood there. "Are you alright?" he asked.

"Sure," Ki nodded. "You?"

Russell walked right up to him and touched his arm. "What is it? You look pale. Come sit down."

Joby nodded. He walked over and sat next to Ki on the sofa. "I need to tell you guys something."

"What?"

"Tenshi warned me this could happen when he broke the rules."

"You seem pretty tight with Tenshi," Ki muttered.

He nodded. "I'm his soldier here on Earth."

"Soldier?" the two men echoed together.

"I am the one who watches over all the men that come back, make sure they want for nothing, make sure they are alright."

"For a vampire, he's very . . ." Ki began.

"Tenshi is not technically a vampire," Joby looked at Ki. "He is, but before that, he was an angel, stolen by Kenshen."

"Who is Kenshen?" Russell asked.

"Up to a little while ago, he was the one who sleeps. Tenshi took his place and for hundreds of years, he has been searching for Shuguy, his one true love. I now believe that Feng is Shuguy."

"Wait," Russell shook his head. "How?"

"As an angel, Tenshi had power over souls. When he killed Shuguy, he sent his soul into orbit. Which meant at any time, it would be . . . I don't know . . . recycled so to speak."

"Reincarnation," Ki said.

"Exactly," Joby nodded. "Kenshen knows that Shuguy and Tenshi have been reunited. He has awakened and he will destroy them before he lets Shuguy have Tenshi. Then," Joby looked at both men, "he will wipe out mortals and rule again."

"Feng," Russell closed his eyes. "He's in danger."

"He's in the safest place he can be. He's with Tenshi."

"Are you sure?" Ki probed.

Joby nodded. "It's why Kenshen is walking."

"Can we save Vincent?" Ki asked.

"Hopefully," Joby replied. "Only Tenshi has that power."

"What do we do?" Russell asked.

"We wait," he said. "Tenshi will call if he needs me."

"Ah . . . Joby, can I ask you something?" Russell looked at him.

"Sure," he smiled.

"Are you . . . mortal?"

"Kind of."

"What do you mean kind of?"

"My soul continues to be recycled but I live a normal lifespan."

"Does Tenshi know you dress up like women and dance?" Ki giggled.

"I have to," he said. "Sometimes I'm recycled as female. Satisfies an itch I have, yet the heels are a killer."

Russell grinned at him. God, he was in love.

"Do you remember what happened then?" Tenshi asked.

Feng swallowed hard. He was trembling. Tenshi placed an arm around him and held him close.

"I was led into this room. I saw you. Your eyes were red, your teeth . . . it was horrible. I'd been badly beaten, the blood congealing around my wounds. You looked like a wild beast, snarling. You wanted to rip me apart."

Tenshi said nothing. The scene floated in front of his eyes as if it was yesterday. Bloodthirsty, and desperate, he attacked, his teeth ripping at Shuguy's throat as blood rushed into his mouth. He mounted him and sliced up inside of him, holding him prone as he raped him and drank.

Shuguy's pulse slowed, Tenshi humped his passion into him and cried in his neck. *I love you. You will come back to me. Your soul will live eternal.* At that moment, the life left Shuguy's body. He was pulled away, covered in Shuguy's blood, and swept into the arms of a monster but with his secret intact. One day, he would see his Shuguy again.

And the day had arrived. He stood in front of him in human form, in the form of Feng. Tenshi gently stroked his hair and kissed his lips. "He's coming," he whispered.

"And we die all over again," Feng wept.

Tenshi shook his head. "Not this time."

Joby showed Ki to a room where he could sleep and told him not to worry while Russell paced downstairs.

"It will all be over soon."

Russell looked up as he came down the steps. The words brought comfort. "That's a nice thought."

"Um," he nodded.

"How is Ki's headache?"

"It's just stress."

"Sit with me," Russell pleaded. "Talk to me."

"You haven't been watching the news again?" He lifted an eyebrow.

"No." He sighed.

They sat together on the sofa. Joby had changed into jeans and a t-shirt. What a body. What he wouldn't give right now to see him naked.

He tried to focus on something else. "Tell me about you, Joby."

"Nothing much to tell. What do you want to know?"

"How did you become what you are?"

"Well, after Tenshi was stolen, some people formed a group devoted to restoring Tenshi to his rightful place."

"Is it Heaven?"

"Not really as you know Heaven. It's a good place, spirits . . . some say angels, are chosen to look after things. Tenshi was one of those. Although there is a debate over which one. I contend Tenshi was the spirit of peace because of all the wars that have happened over time. I believe that if Tenshi hadn't been stolen, there would have been far less of them."

"And how did this group mean to return Tenshi?"

"They hoped to reverse the vampire curse, thinking that if Tenshi was once again the way he was, he would be taken back to his place."

"Can it be reversed?"

"I don't think so."

"But you are his right-hand man or woman . . . so to speak, right?" Russell asked.

"Yes." He nodded. "I guide the ones he returns."

Russell met his eyes. "You're beautiful. Has Tenshi taken you as a lover?"

He smiled faintly. "Of course."

"And you were never his chosen one?"

"Russell, his chosen one has always been Shuguy. No one could have competed with that."

"Are you in love with . . . Tenshi?" Russell swallowed.

"Aren't you, a little?"

Russell smiled.

"I'm the same. It's doesn't mean I can't find real . . . well . . . love." He licked his lips.

"Is it hot in here?" Russell asked, squirming a little.

"No, but you're hot," Joby told him.

Russell met his eyes. "Will you do me a favor?"

"Anything."

"Take off your clothes."

He laughed. "That's quite a request."

"Please?"

Joby began to undo his shirt. "Fast or slow?"

"As quick as possible."

He grinned. "My pleasure."

"How long do we have?" Feng asked undoing Tenshi's shirt.

"Long enough to make love," he whispered, kissing along Feng's neck.

"I want to be with your forever."

"You will be," he groaned as Feng kissed across his chest and pushed his chest away. He let his mind image a beautiful room with a huge bed and a breeze blowing. He led Feng to the bed.

"How did you do that?" Feng smiled.

"Because you wanted it."

Feng clung to him, undoing his pants, and hitching them down.

Tenshi wasted no time. He stripped off Feng's clothes, along with his own, and took Feng down with him on the bed. Hot kisses and roving hands had them both moaning with need. Tenshi lifted Feng high over his hips with one hand, lubricating his entrance with his finger as Feng began to move up and down on it. "I want your cock," he pleaded.

"Take it," Tenshi invited, positioning his hard organ so that Feng could lower himself on it.

"Ooh, that's so good," Feng moaned. "You spread me so wide, so deep . . . like at the wall."

"Yes, my love," he whispered, his head going back, blood tears collecting in his eyes as he remembered.

Feng lifted with his knees, riding him hard, half-way out then full throttle in again. Tenshi cried out.

Feng reached out to rub Tenshi's chest, stimulate his nipples as he fucked himself hard on Tenshi's organ. *My love. We'll be together forever. My angel. Oh yessss! Yessss!*

The memories of that dark somber place flooded over him as his body shuddered with orgasm and Tenshi collected him in his arms. He knew what had to happen and he wanted it. "You would have done it that night if you'd had the chance."

"Yes. I could only send your soul away. That was my only hope. If I had attempted to make you immortal, he would have killed us both."

Feng offered his throat. "Drink."

Tenshi's fangs appeared but Feng felt no fear. The teeth sank deep into his throat and he lay silently, cherishing his nearness. His pulse slowed then his heartbeat and he felt himself fading. The last thing he remembered was being bent over the wall with Tenshi moving inside of him. *Um. So sexy, so beautiful, so . . . pleasurable.*

Russell reached out and caught Joby's erection in his hand, pulling him closer. "Nice cock," he said.

"Thank you," he replied.

"Will you dress up for me?" Russell asked, finally thinking how the thought would turn him on big time.

"Come upstairs," he motioned with his hand.

Russell followed him like a zombie.

"Strip down and lay on the bed," Joby told him, closing the door.

Russell eagerly obeyed. He was stroking himself when Joby disappeared into the adjoining room. He needed this. His stress level was at an all-time high. Hell, the world could turn upside down at any minute.

The door opened and Joby appeared. He was wearing six-inch stilettos, a pair of silk crotchless panties with his erect cock exposed, a garter belt with sexy black hose and two gold clamps on his perfect nipples.

"Turn around," Russell breathed.

His perfect ass was visible thought the sheerness of his see-through lace panties.

"You like?" He licked his lips.

"I'm feeling very randy. How about some really rough sex, baby? No pain, just play?"

Joby winked. "Bring it on, big fellow."

Tenshi stood in front of an unconscious Feng. If he didn't give him blood soon, he was going to die. Kenshen faced him in the image of Vincent. His face was filled with anger and vengeance. "You betrayed me. Let him die and I'll forgive you."

"No."

"I will destroy you both."

"You can try," Tenshi replied.

"You can't defeat me."

"Watch me."

Vincent took a step. "Remember what we shared."

"I remember only pain."

"I gave you joy."

"You tried to possess me. You stole me from my rightful place and gave me this curse. I should have destroyed you while I had the chance."

"But you didn't. The angel in you wouldn't let it be."

"I've long forgotten that." Tenshi rose up off the earth. "Michael was an angel too . . . he took down his enemies with a sword. I have this," he said, withdrawing the Phurpa.

Kenshen took step back.

Tenshi smiled.

"It is the original, isn't it?"

"Yes," he nodded. "It's called a magic dagger, but with its triple blade, it's more of a peg than anything else, a tantric, ritual object used to conquer evil spirits. This is going to hurt because not only will it stab you, it's going to bind you forever."

"You remember."

"I do," he nodded. "The triple blades represent the cutting through of three poisons, ignorance, desire and hatred. It also represents control over the three times of the past, present and future. And it's an instrument of wrath. You see the triangular shape," Tenshi caressed it, "it represents fire and revenge. I've waited so long."

"You must have great Karma, concentration and ability to wield." He laughed.

"You may laugh if you like," Tenshi's expression

hardened. "I was a good scholar. I learned my lessons well. Goodbye, Kenshen." Tenshi threw the dagger, imagining he was destroying all evil in its wake.

It pierced Kenshen's heart. He went to his knees, held out his hand. Tenshi felt the curse leaving and he turned, panicked. "No." He ran to Feng, who was near the brink of death and bit into his own arm. He held his arm to Feng's lips. "Drink. Drink my love before it's too late."

Joby knelt on the bed on his hands and knees, with nothing on now but those red high heels. Russell never would have thought he'd be so turned on by a man in heels. Peeling off the stocking and panties had been fun. He'd kept the clamps and used a big sex toy to loosen Joby up. He still played with the sex toy as he pushed Joby up on his knees and reached around to mess with the clamps. "I think you're going to suck me," Russell demanded. Russell sat on the end of the bed. "Stand up and get over here. Leave the sex toy in your ass."

Joby grinned at him, walking perfectly in those heels. "Ooh, so demanding."

Russell grinned. "On your knees."

Joby dropped in front of him and began to suck him.

"Very, very nice." Russell let it go on until he was sure he was going to come. "Okay, um . . . stop."

Joby looked up at him, his mouth slick with Russell's juices.

"On the floor. I'm going to take you on the floor."

Russell took a minute to look at him on his knees, sex toy still inside of him, at those red shoes. "Baby," he whispered, getting behind him. He stroked his hair and spanked him a few times. Then he moved the toy in and out and threw it aside. Joby groaned. Russell told himself he could hold off. He wanted to play. "Roll over," he instructed.

Joby lay on his back. "What a body you got." Russell pulled on the clamps and cuffed his erection a few times. He kissed his mouth tenderly then pulled off the clamps, licking and suckling his nipples. He took his cock in hand and stroked it.

Joby was thrashing and pleaded.

"Quiet," he said, stroking him more, cupping his balls.

"Please."

"Spread your legs and lift them. I want to see that ... .glory ... um ... nice and spread now. Ready." Russell put two fingers up inside of him and moved them around.

Joby was breathing hard.

Russell held his legs high and drilled into him hard, his hand feeling for one of those shoes. "So sexy," he grunted. "Joby ... damn ... I love you." He slammed him hard and Joby moaned with pleasure. "Harder!" he cried. Damn, Russell thought, he'd just found his perfect match. Only problem was, he wasn't going to want to do anything except dress up his doll and fuck him good every minute of the day. YUM!

CHAPTER SIX

His body was changing and changing fast. Tenshi wasn't sure what would happen when the transformation was complete. Kenshen was no more. The dagger had entered him, and he had fallen forward on his face, and disintegrated.

Joby stood at his side looking down at Feng. "I'm sure you got him in time," he said, touching Tenshi's arm.

"Thank you for answering my call so quickly. I didn't have the strength to bring him here myself."

Joby smiled. "That's what I'm here for, eternally. Are you scared?"

He nodded. "A little. I'm not scared of death." He walked over to the window and looked out. "I'm scared of leaving him." He glanced over at Feng. "All this time. Finally, we're together again and now this."

"Why do you think it's happening? Is it because Kenshen is gone?"

Tenshi nodded. "I believe so. How is Vincent?"

"Confused more than anything. He doesn't remember any of it."

"He might eventually. He remembered me. Of course, I am unforgettable."

"Did you say you were an angel?"

He laughed. "Always a bit of a devil thrown in for good measure."

Joby chuckled.

Tenshi kissed him on top of the head. "Don't change. Stay exactly how you are. And ah . . . who have you been . . ."

"You can smell that?"

"Of course."

Joby raised his eyebrows. "I'll never tell. I could be in love."

"If you are then . . ."

"Tenshi," Feng cried out from the bed.

Tenshi rushed over. "Feng. Feng? Are you alright?"

"I feel . . . funny."

Tenshi sat beside him, held his hand. "You'll be fine. I'll teach you . . . I'll . . ." Suddenly he was gripped with pain. He doubled over, fell on the floor.

Joby ran to him.

Feng sat up. "What's wrong with him? What's happening?"

Joby looked up at Feng with tears in his eyes. "He's dying."

Russell came running into the room now. He'd just woken up and spoke to Ki. Vincent was fine, just confused but he said that Feng was unconscious. He was surprised to see Tenshi on the floor.

"Help me," Roby said to Russell. "We need to lay him down."

They got him to a bed. Feng came with them, staggering as if drunk. "Feng, are you alright?" Russell asked as Joby leaned over Tenshi.

Two bright red tears ran down Feng's cheeks. "He's dying."

"What to . . . Feng," Russell backed away, "you're a . . . a . . . vampire."

Feng wasn't listening. He went to Tenshi's side. "You've got to save him, Joby. Do whatever it takes."

Joby stood. He looked at Russell. "Go out to the desert and get me some ghost flowers."

"Ghost flowers? Why?"

"Because maybe I can save him," Joby said. "Hurry, he doesn't have long. And while you're at it, go downstairs to the fridge and bring Feng some blood. I don't fancy being his breakfast."

Russell grinned and kissed his cheek. "Now you're bossing me around?"

"You only get to be my master in bed, honey, don't you forget it."

"I'll just have to content myself with that. So . . . ah . . . how many of these flowers do we need?"

"Only one."

"Okay."

As Feng drank the blood, it felt amazingly normal, although the look of it kind of freaked him out. He stayed close to Tenshi. He'd tried feeding him his blood, but he wouldn't take it, or he couldn't.

"He has a pulse," Joby said, shaking his head.

"He's mortal then?"

Joby nodded.

"It makes no sense. He wasn't mortal to begin with."

"I have a feeling the transformation is not complete."

Feng stroked Tenshi's face. "And the ghost flower is for what?"

"When Kenshen first saw Tenshi, he saw purity. He wanted to taint his purity with his blood, corrupt innocence. Out of that, came the ghost flower."

"Then Kenshen created these flowers?"

"In a sense."

"Why are they here in California?"

"Because of you, I suppose."

"This flower will save him?"

"I've consulted with the others. They tell me I'm doing right. Feng, I don't know what it will do, but it's meant to be."

Feng began to cry again. "I can't lose him."

Joby squeezed his arm. "Stay close to him. He knows

75

you're here."

The wait for Russell to return seemed endless. Ki and Vincent came into the room, arm and arm, but they seemed a little nervous around him. "I won't hurt you," he said. Even that seemed strange.

"Are you and Vincent . . . a couple?" Feng asked curiously.

Vincent hugged Ki. "I could live with that."

Ki pushed him off playfully with a big grin. "Down boy."

Feng saw where that was going. Just like Russell. There was a spark in his eye when he looked at Joby, and who could blame him, that boy was hot!

When Russell rushed in with the flower, Joby told Feng to back away.

"What are you going to do?" Feng demanded.

Russell pulled him back. "Just let him do it."

Joby ripped the petals from the flower and threw it in the air over Tenshi. They landed on the blanket. Feng watched anxiously but nothing happened. Tenshi didn't move. He was about to say something when Joby cried out some words which somehow Feng understood.

Joby called out, "Deliver him. Right the wrongs that were done and bring peace!"

Suddenly they all stood back, a collective gasp going through the room as a pure white angel rose out of Tenshi's body. His face was beautiful, his body, perfect. It was Tenshi. He floated up and disappeared.

"No, no!" Feng cried out. "You said you'd save him," he screamed at Joby. "He's gone from me forever. He's . . ."

"Feng?"

Feng froze and turned around. Tenshi sat up in bed, smiling. "Stop yelling. I'm here."

Feng ran over to the bed and hugged him. "Baby, baby, are you alright? What happened? I saw you go and . . ."

"It was my spirit, a spirit of the past. A spirit I will eventually return to, but only when I die a natural death." He looked over at Joby and smiled. "You released me with the flower. Thanks."

Joby nodded. He pushed everyone from the room. "A little privacy," he said, closing the door.

Feng backed off from him a little. "Tenshi?"

"Um?"

"You're mortal."

He nodded. "Yes. My reprieve until I return to my angelic form. But they've given me an entire lifetime."

Feng felt his sharp teeth thoughtfully. "And ironically, I'm not."

"I'm sorry. I had no choice. He would have killed you."

"I don't blame you. In fact," he grinned, "could be fun."

"As long as you control it."

"You'll help me."

"I dare say. I can relate."

Feng shook his head, the fear claiming him again. "This is . . . a little crazy."

"We're together. It doesn't matter what you are, Feng. I love you."

Feng pressed his forehead to his. "I love you. I've loved you forever. Should I make you like me then?"

Tenshi considered that for a moment. "No. I can't. I must be who I was meant to be. I must live out a mortal life to do that." He drew Feng down into his arms. "It will be alright."

Feng nodded as he kissed him passionately. His desire and his thirst for blood rose together. As his jaw opened, he lowered his teeth to Tenshi's throat but for some reason, he couldn't bite down. He looked at him.

Tenshi smiled.

"I . . . lost control. I wanted to . . . but I couldn't."

"I said I was mortal. I didn't say I was completely without

any powers." He grinned and took Feng down in the bed, kissing and undressing as he went. "I was an angel, remember?"

Feng licked his lips and pushed his hips upwards with a moan. Angel or devil, Tenshi was turning him on big time. "I love you, angel," he whispered but Tenshi didn't hear him. He was busy elsewhere.

ABOUT THE AUTHOR

A.J. Llewellyn is the author of almost three hundred published gay romance novels. A.J. lives in California, but dreams of living in Hawaii. Frequent trips to all the islands, bags of Kona coffee in the fridge and a healthy collection of Hawaiian records keep A.J. refueled.

A.J's passion for the islands led to writing a play about the last ruling monarch of Hawaii, Queen Lili'uokalani. A.J. has written a non-erotic novel about the overthrow of her kingdom written in diary form from her maid's point of view.

A.J. never lacks inspiration for male/male erotic romances and has to prise fingers from the computer keyboard to pursue other passions: collecting books on Hawaiiana, surfing and spending time with family, friends and animal companions.

D.J. Manly: I write not only for my own pleasure but for the pleasure of my readers. I can't remember a time in my life when I haven't written and told stories. When I'm not writing, I'm dreaming about writing, doing something wild and adventurous, or trying to make the world a better and more open-minded place to live in. I adore beautiful men, and I know I'm not alone in this! Eroticism between consenting adults, in all its many forms, is the icing on the cake of life!

D.J. has published well over two hundred novels/novellas and is a well-seasoned writer.

www.ingramcontent.com/pod-product-compliance
Lightning Source LLC
Chambersburg PA
CBHW071126130626
46555CB00010B/1452